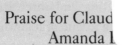

Also by Claudia Mair Burney

*Deadly Charm**
Wounded: A Love Story
*Death, Deceit & Some Smooth Jazz**
Zora & Nicky: A Novel in Black & White
*Murder, Mayhem & a Fine Man**
Always Sisters (with CeCe Winans)

Also in the Exorsistah series

*The Exorsistah**
*The Exorsistah: X Returns**

*Also available from Simon & Schuster

CLAUDIA MAIR BURNEY

THE EXORSISTAH:

X
RESTORED

POCKET STAR BOOKS

New York   London   Toronto   Sydney

Pocket Star Books
A Division of Simon & Schuster, Inc.
1230 Avenue of the Americas
New York, NY 10020

This book is a work of fiction. Names, characters, places, and incidents either are products of the author's imagination or are used fictitiously. Any resemblance to actual events or locales or persons, living or dead, is entirely coincidental.

First Pocket Star Books paperback edition June 2011

POCKET STAR BOOKS and colophon are registered trademarks of Simon & Schuster, Inc.

For information about special discounts for bulk purchases, please contact Simon & Schuster Special Sales at 1-866-506-1949 or business@simonandschuster.com.

The Simon & Schuster Speakers Bureau can bring authors to your live event. For more information or to book an event contact the Simon & Schuster Speakers Bureau at 1-866-248-3049 or visit our website at www.simonspeakers.com.

Cover design by Anna Dorfman, photo by James Steidl/Shutterstock

Manufactured in the United States of America

10 9 8 7 6 5 4 3 2 1

ISBN 978-1-4165-6135-4
ISBN 978-1-4391-7682-5 (ebook)

For Bianca, the child of my heart,
and to
Heather Diane Tipton, the friend of my soul.

Daughter to Mother

Well, Mama, I'll tell you:
Life for me ain't been no crystal stair.
It's been sole-bloodying roads,
Dangerous and cold
To destinations I shouldn't have traveled
Alone.
But all the time
I kept on goin'.
Hurtin'.
Tears flowin'.
Every step I took, I did so
Knowin,' if I searched the darkest lands
Where there ain't never been no light,
I just might find you reaching for my hands.
I had to sit a few times, Mama.
Sometimes the road was kinda hard.
But I got up running; I had to get to where you are.
I'm still going, Mama.
I'm almost there
Though life for me ain't been no crystal stair.

Chapter One

I hate demons," I said to Francis. With a whap I slammed my journal shut. "They inspire bad poetry."

"Among other things," he said with a wry smile. He kept his eyes fixed on the road as we zoomed down Interstate 10. We were on our way to New Orleans to see my mama. Finally. It had been three long years. Nerves stirred my insides like the agitator inside a washing machine.

"Don't get me started on John 10:10," I ranted.

"It says, 'The thief comes only to steal, kill, and destroy.' And his triflin' minions never let up. They possess the people you love, attach themselves to you, and ruin your relationships."

"I won't get you started on that."

"Did I mention they inspire bad poetry?"

"As a matter of fact you did. What's wrong with your poem, baby?"

"Besides *everything*, it's whiny. Mama's going to hate it. And could you please tell me why I took on Langston Hughes?"

"It's not like you challenged him to a rap battle, Emme. You flipped his poem, which is a fierce way to express how hard your journey has been. I dug it. Your *madre* will, too."

"But 'Mother to Son' is perfect."

"I'm gonna take a wild guess and say Langston Hughes probably revised his work. Give yourself time. You just wrote that half a mile back."

"It's hopeless." What I meant was *I* was hopeless.

"Not much in this world is hopeless, and certainly not you." Francis said. "This trip alone should show you that much."

It should have. I was going to be with my mama! In no time I'd have my arms around her, snottin' and crying my fool head off, but painful memories of her collided with my hope. It was hard to focus on anything beyond how unpredictable life could be.

I yanked the visor down for an umpteenth look in the mirror and groaned at my reflection. My fitful sleep the night before had left my dark skin dull. Combined with my stark white hair, drooping in ropy lengths down my back, a sistah looked downright ghastly. Francis's voice penetrated my self-loathing, and I snapped the visor back up.

"Talk to me, X. And don't tell me you're upset about your poem."

"I'm fine," I mumbled, crossing my arms over my chest.

"Oh, I know you're fine, but what's the matter?"

A smile tugged at the corners of my mouth. "Dude! That was, like, the lamest line ever." But the furious blush rising in my cheeks contradicted my words.

His laughter fell on my ears like music. "Yeah, but it coaxed you out of your blues. Don't sleep on a brotha's skills in the art of seduction."

"That was you seducing me?"

"That was me reminding you that there's more to your beauty than what you see in the mirror. I'll do the seducing on our wedding night."

"You're the one who's fine, Francis. And I'm not just talking about your looks."

Red stole up Francis's neck, and he flashed that

rare, single dimple at me. I love to see him flushed; it actually makes him prettier. His skin is the color of cocoa, with a florid hue beneath that hot chocolate, courtesy of his Latino dad. He blushes and his cheeks bloom roses. Flecks of gold illuminate his liquid light brown eyes. One sultry look from him *kills* me.

"I wouldn't mind taking in more of the view over there," Francis said, his eyes sweeping over me before he turned back to watch the road. "Unfortunately, I'm driving. I'll have to settle for looking at this beautiful countryside."

Once again, I turned my gaze to the window to see the strange new world that was Louisiana. Exotic vegetation—some of it still lush in December—flourished beside bridge-covered swamps. Centuries-old cypress trees wrapped in Spanish moss stood like sentries next to massive oaks, their bark blackened with age. Now and then we'd pass plantation houses towering in the distance. It was like we were driving right into the setting of an Anne Rice novel. How soon, I wondered, would the creatures of the night show up?

Which made me think of demons, which prompted the unsettling memories of the worst times with Mama, and again I teetered on the edge of an abyss of worry.

"Emme, baby?" Francis cooed, his voice as sweet as honey.

"I'm all right, Francesco."

"Yes, you are. If only *you* could believe it when you say it. Because it really is all good, baby. The worst is over. You made it though all your trials, tribulations, tests, and even temptations, stronger than you were before."

I nodded and raked my fingers through my blanched tresses, now aware of my stupid white hair. "Dang it."

"What?"

"How am I supposed to explain the Storm look to my mama?"

"Tell her what I always say: you're a superhero now."

"She ain't into Marvel comics."

"It doesn't matter, because you aren't Storm. You're the *Exorsistah*! I'll bet she'll understand that! Anyway, she won't care what color your hair is. She'll just be glad to hug your neck."

I stared out of the window again, saying nothing.

"You don't have to torture yourself, X. For the hundredth time, everything is going to be great."

And for the hundredth time, I wished I could be sure.

A dense white fog had rolled in from the Gulf,

bringing with it a rare flurry of snowflakes. I felt as scattered as the fragile bits of white falling from it. "How far are we from New Orleans?"

"Less than thirty miles." He reached over and gave my hand a quick squeeze. I'd have paid good money for that gesture to give me just the tiniest measure of deep-down-in-my-soul certainty. But I got nothin'.

"Trust God on this," Francis said, discerning my thoughts in that maddening way he does. "He's not going to disappoint you."

Francis is what you call a "sensitive." He can *feel* what's happening in the spirit realm. You know that phrase, "touch and agree" in prayer? We did that once and meshed souls irrevocably. There are times when my gift becomes his, and his mine: I can feel what he feels, and he can see what I see like we're a couple of empaths, only we're fine-tuned to each other. On several occasions the simple sensation of his hand in mine was enough to give me all the reassurance I needed.

"I don't have to be an empath to get what's bothering you," Francis said.

"Dude! You pulled that word right out of my brain!"

"It's so much nicer talking to you."

Resistance was futile. Francis was capable of

traipsing through my mind like we were part of the Borg Collective sometimes. I decided to get it over with and talk to him.

"I'm afraid to see her."

He kept his eyes steady on the road. "That's exactly how I felt before I met Father Miguel." Francis chuckled and shook his head. "I went through a *thang*, baby. I had all these ideas about what he'd be like. My personal favorite was gruff, good-looking priest, right out of a Hollywood movie. Like Antonio Banderas in a Roman collar! But when I knocked on the door some old dude answered who looked like he could be my grandfather." He paused, suddenly pensive. "But I saw my own face in his. It amazed me. I was so shocked I blurted out, 'My mama said you my daddy.'"

Now his raucous laughter filled the car. "All the color drained from his face. I'm surprised he didn't throw holy water on me."

"Father Miguel was an exorcist. He'd seen worse than you."

"Oh, I surprised him, baby. *Trust.*"

"What did he say?"

"I don't know. I didn't speak Spanish yet, but I guessed that he didn't believe me, which he later confirmed. Repeatedly."

"What did you do?"

"Later, I took the DNA test he insisted on, but I was mad about it, and I stayed mad for the next three years: at my mother for dying, at God for taking her, and now that I think of it, I was angry at myself for needing my father, but it was just grief, Emme." His expression turned somber. "So much of grief is anger, or fear, but they feel a lot worse than being sad does. Don't waste the moments you'll have with your mother acting a fool. Time goes by too fast. You'll look up, and she'll be gone again."

Father Miguel had died a little over a week before. I leaned over and kissed Francis's cheek. "I'll try my best. Thank you for driving me. You should be back in Inkster dealing with your loss instead of running me a thousand miles down the road."

"I'd rather be here than there, crying all over my bass guitar."

"Have I told you lately that you're wonderful?"

"Say it another couple of thousand times, and I might start to believe you."

"At least you didn't leave your dad to languish in a mental hospital."

"You were a kid, Emme. Your mother will understand the choices you had to make."

"She would have done things differently."

"How do you know that?"

"Because I have my own paternity surprise." I

took a deep breath and let it out. "Miss Jane told me I was a rape baby. I never knew before then." Miss Jane was the surprising mystic who sent Francis and I on this journey. She was also the original Exorsistah who delivered my mother from demons. Miss Jane was full of unsettling surprises, and although she had gone to be with the Lord right after Francis's dad, I was sure somehow she'd have a few more for me.

Francis's mouth opened, then closed again, not a word coming out. An endless minute passed before he finally spoke. "Your *madre* was raped? I'm sorry to hear it. That's heavy, X."

"Heavy ain't the word for it."

Anxiety clutched me again, turning quickly into an impending sense of doom. The word "heavy" seemed to hang in the air like the Acme anvil in Road Runner cartoons, about to drop on my head. I could feel it closing in on me until it crushed my skull; an instant migraine seemed to split my head in two.

Perspiration moistened my skin, and my breath came in ragged gasps. The oppressive heat inside the car made me fumble for the power window button, but I couldn't find it to save my life. Francis pushed it from the driver's side, and a blast of cool, moist air hit me in the face.

But wheezing burned my lungs, and a sharp pain

seized my chest. Confusion scrambled my thoughts. I couldn't focus enough to form the words "Help me."

I'd fought a lot of demons in my day, big, bad, nasty demons, but I'd never encountered anything like the terrifying heaviness squeezing the life out of me. Tears bit at my eyes. Whatever was happening was going kill me, and I had no idea why. The last thing I remember was grabbing Francis's shirt. Then everything went black.

Chapter Two

I woke up in Francis's arms to the sound of his prayers washing over me. He had pulled over to the side of the road. The window was still open, and the wind whipping through chilled me to the bone. Shudders rippled through my body.

With the kind of gentleness that had made me fall in love with him, Francis rubbed up and down my arms and cradled my face in his hands.

"Welcome back, baby."

"OMGosh! What happened? I thought I was

dying. What kind of freakin' demonless demon attack was that?"

"It wasn't demonic, baby. I think you had a panic attack."

"A *panic attack*? Emme Vaughn does not have panic attacks!"

"I used to have them myself. They were worse right before I met my father."

"Oh heck-e-naw!" I shook my head so hard I could have rattled my brain. "I ain't goin' out like that!" Tears slid out of my traitor eyes, and I swiped at them hard with the back of my hands. I felt like my body had betrayed me, that I had no control over it anymore.

"It's okay," Francis crooned, wiping my eyes with the pads of his thumbs. "Just relax." He yanked the bottom of his black turtleneck out of his waistband and held my hand to his bare chest. "Get lost in my rhythm, like my heartbeat is the only thing in the world."

I folded into Francis's welcoming arms, laying both palms flat on his broad chest. His warmth enveloped me and the *thumpbump*, *thumpbump*, *thumpbump* of his heart anchored me to him. Soon my breath steadied, flowing in and out of my lungs in sync with his. I rested on him until I felt more together, then reluctantly pulled away.

"We don't have to rush," he said. "You can stay here for as long as you want."

"I'm ready to go," I lied. The truth was my meltdown embarrassed me. I'd been weak, and Emme Vaughn couldn't afford such a luxury. If demons were watching—and I could count on the fact that they were—they'd use that information against me and whoop all over my head.

"I can't let that happen again, Francis. I go to war with the powers of darkness. If I lose my mind at the prospect of seeing my mama, I might as well turn in my diva boots now."

"Keep those stilettos on, baby. I promise you're gonna need 'em. It ain't over until it's over, and trust, demons aren't the only things in life that are scary." His golden eyes brightened. "Tell you what. How 'bout we make the French Quarter our playground tonight? We'll stop at the St. Louis Cathedral to pray before we play. You haven't seen a church till you've see this one. After that we can have a *réveillon*. It's Christmastime in N'awlins, and Papa Noel and the Christ Child are generous tonight. If you feel like it, after dinner we can go dancing, then retire to a fine hotel. No more Motel Six! And after you've had a good night's sleep you can put your courage on and we'll go see your mother, but for now, all you have to do is hang with yo' boy. Bet?"

A goofy grin spread across my face. "Bet!"

Francis gave me a little more time to collect myself before he merged us back into traffic. Twenty minutes passed like five and Francis turned onto South Claiborne Avenue. I read the blue and gold greeting, with the requisite fleur-de-lis embellishment: "Welcome to New Orleans. Downtown!"

"*Bienvenu!*" Francis said. "That means 'welcome' in Creole."

"Dude! You speak ghetto Spanglish *and* Creole?"

His laughter affirmed that my baby indeed knew how to talk that talk.

Excitement, the good kind, rose in me. The city was adorned in Christmas finery. Glowing white lights snaked up and down palm trees and old-fashioned iron street lamps, while red-bowed wreaths brought cheer to the shop doorways.

"Wait till you see the French Quarter," Francis said, beaming. "We'll be there in about four minutes, *mon amour chéri.*"

"*Mon amour chéri?*"

"My cherished love. We're in N'awlins now. Gotta talk like the natives."

"What do I call you?"

"You can call me *mon papé*, your daddy. "

I cracked up, but before I could get *mon papé*

out of my mouth, my breath caught. A girl, no older than me, appeared in our path. Blood had ruined her lovely white formal gown. Her reddish brown hair fell in waves to her slit throat, slashed so deeply she had to hold up her head with one hand. The other flicked a wave at me. Francis was going to mow her down.

I grabbed the dashboard to brace myself for the impact, but he drove right through her, oblivious. I whipped my head around to see if she still stood there, but she had vanished.

Chapter Three

D ude!" I screeched.

"What?"

I had to wait until my heart rate slowed.

I hate seeing the dead! If I never saw another entity, of any kind, when the veil between the seen and unseen world is lifted, I wouldn't be mad about it. The dead don't come with instructions either, and what's worse, the last couple of ghosts I saw made demands. At least I knew who those spirits were. I had no idea who the poor girl we'd passed through was, or what she'd insist upon. I suspected the price of helping her would exceed what I could afford to pay.

That migraine leftover from the panic attack battered my temples anew.

Francis looked at me like I was acting as crazy as I was. "You okay?"

"Yeah. I thought you were about to hit something."

"Hit what?"

"Never mind. My bad." I forced a cleansing breath out of my lungs and slumped back into my seat.

"*Ça k'ap rivé, ma chère,*" Francis said, then translated: "What's happening?"

"Nothing."

"Don't tell me it's nothing, Emme."

"I give you everything I have eventually, don't I, Francis?"

"Eventually."

"Then let it go for now. How do you say 'my head is killing me' in Creole?"

"*Mon latét ap tchué mon!*"

I cocked my head. "Are you serious?"

His solitary dimple winked at me. "I had a couple of migraines the last time I was here." He pointed at the dash. "I've got some Quick Tabs in the glove box. You don't even need water to take 'em. Pop a couple of those. I want you to feel better so I can show you my favorite city."

I stuck two of the tablets in my mouth. As they dissolved, Francis brightened like the Christmas decorations outside. If he didn't tell me about New Orleans he was going to explode.

"All right, *mon papé*. Let me have it."

"New Orleans is awesome." The words seemed to burst out of his body. "It's a feast for your senses. Everything is here: music, food, art, culture, romance, and the Saints, baby! And I ain't talking about the ones in heaven."

"Who dat? What dat?" I chanted. "Who dat say dey gon' beat dem Saints?"

"Yeah, baby! Who. Dat. Nation!"

After our love song to the football team, Francis proceeded to wax eloquent about his beloved New Orleans, his voice swelling with passion. Soon he'd turn his intuition back to my vision, but the distraction of the Big Easy bought me time. Besides, his enthusiasm was contagious, and I let his delight in the city shield me from the brewing trouble.

I stuck my head out the window and took a big whiff of the city. The air smelled like fish, food, and bodies—with a hint of garbage—but man, oh, man! It teemed with energy.

NOLA was a colorful collision of the old and new. Horse-drawn carriages ambled down brick streets, passing banging new jazz joints. The exquisite artistry of the iron lace balconies called galleries— *gul-RAYS*—bewitched me. Old-school charm cohabited with new hotness in a dizzying array of restaurants, antique shops, and boutiques. Funky strains of "When the Saints Go Marching In" poured out of one of the many bars.

"Wicked, isn't it?" Francis asked.

"There's definitely some wickedness," I answered, thinking of the dead girl. The image of her holding her head buzzed through my brain like an electric current.

"What the matter?" Mr. Intuition said.

"My insides are zinging, that's all."

"Mine, too! It happens every time I come here. It's all this tension."

"Tension?"

"This is a thin place, baby, between heaven and hell. And in between you've got your Southern Baptists and Catholics, living side by side with voodoo practitioners and everything else, while south-facing gargoyles and saint and angel statues watch over us all."

"I guess this city has a way of drawing you into its mystery," I said. I meant that literally.

"Are you kidding me? There's more than mystery here. This place is full of magic! It's like the American Venice! Or Paris in the swamps! Baby, this is Africa on the Mississippi! I hit the city limits and it's like coming home. The ancestors whisper to me, and I don't have half your abilities. You must feel haunted in this place."

"Haunted! That is exactly how I feel." I craned my neck to look out the window. "Where's that church you mentioned?"

He chuckled. "Not far at all, Catholic girl. In less than ten minutes we'll be praying in the same place Pope John Paul the Great did."

Francis didn't disappoint me. Soon we were standing in front of the most spectacular edifice I had ever been to. It made All Souls in Inkster look like *The Shack.* The towering white cathedral's multiple spires and central tower—complete with clock and bell—made me think of *The Hunchback of Notre Dame.* Wistful images of the bell ringer, Quasimodo, aflame with love for the gypsy Esmeralda flickered on the movie screen in my imagination. But what snatched my breath away was the statue of Jesus Christ, mounted on the manicured lawn of the back courtyard. He welcomed us with outstretched arms and broken hands.

"What happened to his thumbs, Francis?"

"The hurricane uprooted two huge oak trees in

the courtyard, amputating them, but for all Katrina's fury, the hands were the only part of the statue that was damaged. In his first sermon after the hurricane, the archbishop vowed not to have him fixed until all of New Orleans is healed."

The sentiment made my stomach flutter. Katrina's devastation was evident all around the city, despite massive reconstruction. One or two parish streets upset Francis so much he struggled to hold back tears.

"With your gift you must feel so much mourning," I said.

"Yeah, but I can feel the hope, too. It's a tenacious, crazy hope, but it's here, and it's stronger than the despair."

"It's true." That glorious expectancy throbbed in the zydeco pulse of the city. I linked my arm with Francis's. "Let's go inside."

In the nave we stopped at an elaborate votive-light stand, where Francis stuffed a ten-dollar bill inside the attached offering box. He lit two prayer candles..

"For my *padre*, Father Miguel Rivera, and my *madre*, Francesca Peace. Lord, have mercy on their souls, and grant them peace."

I did the same, only with a few dollar bills.

"Jesus, I pray for my mama, Abigail Vaughn. I'm

so nervous about seeing her. Go before me, Lord, and prepare the way." The second candle was for Jane Doe, my friend and inspiration, in thanksgiving for this journey no matter how weird it was turning out to be. "And this is for Miss Jane. Grant her eternal joy."

We watched the candles flicker. Long after we left, the flames would continue to keep their silent vigil.

Saint Louis's was as lovely inside as it was outside, with a black and white checkered floor, expansive galleries, and a succession of saluting flags. Gold-topped columns rose to a domed ceiling icon of the risen Christ. Emblazoned above his image were the Latin words *Sanctus, Sanctus, Sanctus Dominus Deus Sabaoth.* I knew from hanging out with monks of St. Benedict's Abbey for three months that the words meant "Holy, holy, holy, Lord God of the heavenly hosts."

The church was semicrowded, despite the fact that no Mass was being celebrated, but Francis had told me the St. Louis's offered concerts for the community during the Christmas season. A jazz quartet was due to start soon, so we chose a comfy corner on the back pew. Moments later, I found myself in the lap of silent expectation. The presence of God surrounded me, and with my man hip to hip beside me, my creativity flowed. I pulled my journal out of my purse and jotted down the soul music playing within me.

Thursday evening, 6:45 p.m.
St. Louis Cathedral

HUSH SONG
"Be still and know that I am God." (Psalm 46:10)

be
still

shhsh
what ifs
if onlys
whys
whens

be
quiet

this is the moment of
surrender
hands lifted
fingers unfurled
like petals
in offering

this is before
yes and amen
the quiet fissure
in time/space
between
heaven/hell
that I hide in

breathless moments
make poems worth reading
this is the

space

between the lines

the gaps
that make words of letters

quiet.

Be here
to hear
or . . .

Be quiet:
this is the breath

between annunciation
and conception
of Christ
in you.

Abba singing
His hushsong
saying:

nothing

nothing

sweet nothing.

For a long time we sat in tranquility as soothing as sunset, until Francis grazed my hand to get my attention. I lifted my head to acknowledge his touch, and my heart almost stopped. The dead girl sat right in front of me, one arm flung lazily over the back of the pew.

"*Whoa!*"

My outburst caught a few stares before people went back to their prayers. Francis leaned over and stage-whispered, "Demon?"

I shook my head.

Usually he'd ask for an explanation, but church

etiquette must have restrained him. He made the sign of the cross and went back to praying, but I could tell he'd switched to warfare mode.

While he rebuked the devil, I took in the dead girl. She displayed no mortal wounds this time, appearing otherworldly beautiful. She offered a shy smile; her honey-colored skin shimmering incandescently. When I returned her smile, she extended her hand towards me.

It's one thing to see the dead; it's another to touch them. Not that I had much experience with that.

Francis remained deep in battle, so I looked around the sanctuary, hoping anything would spark some insight. Nada. The girl seemed so sad, and no one appeared to be watching. I cast another surreptitious look her way.

What the heck! I eased my hand toward hers.

Bad. I. De-ah. Her creepy grasp felt almost as substantial as mine. Then *blam!* I don't know what that dead heifer did, but my mood plunged so abruptly I gasped.

Francis put his arm around me. "What's going on, Emme?"

"*Ô, to konnè, tou les jou, la mèm affaire,*" I said, dryly. But I was beginning to feel queasy. I wanted to get of out there, fast.

"*Allons,*" I said.

Francis tilted his head liked I'd suddenly become a stranger. "No problem."

"Mèsi bôcou."

On the way out we stopped at the votive stand again, and I lit a candle for the dead girl. Thank God for sacramentals. I didn't feel quite like myself, and God knew I was at a loss for words to pray.

Francis tried to lighten the tone, but his grin looked forced. "Let the good times roll!" he said.

I shook my head, wearily. *"Non, mèsi."* All I wanted to do was chill in the hotel room he had promised, but Francis looked at me like I'd spoken another language.

Chapter Four

By the time we got to the statue of Jesus a strange coldness had attached itself to me. It wasn't the weather. The temperature lingered in the mid-sixties. This was different. Ominous.

Francis eyed me as warily as I had the dead girl. "Are you all right, Emme?" Anxiety etched itself on his face.

"Yeah. Stop looking at me like that."

"I'm sorry. I'm just surprised. I didn't know you spoke Creole."

"I don't."

"Emme, in the church when I asked you what was going on, you said, 'Same thing, different day' as fluidly as any Louisiana Creole I've ever talked to."

"You're trippin'. I don't even know French."

"Then you said, *'allons':* let's go."

"I said that in English."

"I tested you, Emme. I told you, *'Padèkwa.'* To be sure I added, *'Laissez les bons temps rouler,'* and you answered, 'No, thanks.' In *Creole*."

I didn't know why he was messing with my head, but I didn't like it. "I said no thanks in English. Quit playing, Francis."

"I'm not kidding."

"Then you're delusional."

He looked at me with those luminous gold eyes. "Emme, you were speaking in another language. Are you seriously telling me you were completely unaware of it?"

"What I'm telling you is that you must have it twisted. I spoke to you in plain English, the only language I speak, unless you want to count Ebonics." He stared at me, and I had to wonder if I was doing it again, totally unaware of it.

"What?" I said.

"Maybe you were speaking in tongues, the way they did in the book of Acts. Remember how when the Holy Spirit came over the crowd, they could talk and hear in language they didn't speak." His didactic tone annoyed me.

"Francis," I said slowly, "I've been Charismatic most of my life. I know what tongues are, and I wasn't speaking in them."

"Then what was that all about?"

"It wasn't about anything, since I wasn't doing it in the first place." My hands began to shake, and I put them on my hips to steady them. "I'm not in the mood for your spooky theories, Mulder. So if it isn't happening now—not that it was happening before—I'd like to drop the subject."

"No problem, Scully."

We continued toward his car, but the whole matter nagged at me.

Did I speak in tongues for real? I thought. *I haven't done that in a while, and every time before I had known it was happening.*

My mind went back to dozens of conversations I had with my mother back in the day. She'd say and do all kinds of crazy stuff and five minutes later would have no clue about what happened. That was the beginning of her descent into madness, or what we later found out was demon possession.

Inwardly, I panicked. *Oh, man. Why in the heck did I touch that girl?*

I knew better. The scriptures say to try the spirits to see if they're from God, and there I was reaching out to touch her like she was the Holy Ghost. She could have been pure, unadulterated evil.

But wouldn't I have known that?

I'd seen evil since I was five years old. I'd even seen an angel of light. Those things might dazzle, but they leave you with a weird, unsettled feeling. There's no peace when you see something that's not of God. When the Lord sends something your way, the peace is pervasive. At least that's my experience.

Of course, I couldn't forget the scriptures. How many times had people seen a real live angel of God, and the first thing the angel had to say was, "Fear not"?

What's happening to me?

Sweat beaded on my forehead. I stepped livelier to avoid any more conversation—useless with such a long-legged fiancé. He matched my stride and chattered away, his words sounding like gibberish. We reached the Camry and I had no idea what he had said.

"Emme?" he said, his voice brimming with concern.

"What?"

"I asked you a question. Are you just going to ignore me?"

"Of course not. I was just thinking."

He waited for a moment. The cold clinging to me began to feel like an arctic blast. My teeth chattered.

"Well?" Francis asked, his eyebrows raised.

"What, Francis?"

He sighed, as if he were dealing with a very small child. "What would you like to have for dinner?"

Oh, man. Something was very wrong if I missed a cue to have a meal, or worse, didn't want to go to a restaurant to get it.

"Can we just order in?"

He looked at me incredulously. "In *New Orleans*?"

A shudder quaked through me. "I'm sorry, but I feel so cold. Maybe I'm coming down with something."

"You can have some gumbo. That'll cure whatever ails you, baby."

Except for the melancholy I was experiencing. Sorrow wrapped itself around me like a mummy's burial cloths. "Please, baby. I really don't want to."

"*Mon amour chéri*, this is my joint! Let me take you somewhere amazing to eat."

"I need some rest."

He threw up his hands. "Okay. Rest it is." Francis buttoned my coat and followed that kindness by rubbing my hands in his. I collapsed into the sandalwood and vetiver scenting his neck.

As I clung to him, in that mystifying way we do, we made an exchange. I gave him the nebulous pain flattening me; he bestowed on me some measure of his rock-solid strength. The urge to lose myself in him again almost overpowered me. This time I sought his heartbeat by touching his neck, burrowing my face deeper into his warmth and pressing my lips across the tender flesh where his pulse throbbed. Impulsively, I tasted his rhythm against my tongue. Francis's arms tightened around my waist, and he pulled me closer to him. "Have mercy on a brotha."

But I had none to offer. I pressed my lips against his and slid my tongue into his mouth. My hands tangled in his hair. In his arms I felt a heady blend of pleasure and protection that chased away the fear that dogged me. Kissing him, letting my hands roam his silken, shiny black mane, there was no ghost.

He pushed me away, gently, but his message was firm. "Cool your jets, girl. We're in the parking lot of a church."

I stared at him, confused. "I wanted to get lost in your rhythm again."

"*Mon amour chéri*, there are several ways to get lost in my rhythm, and we ain't tryna go there."

His words, and the shame that followed, sucker-punched me. A sound came out of my mouth: something between "oh" and "ugh," which articulated exactly how much my behavior bewildered and disgusted me.

I wanted to ask Francis to forgive me, but the words wouldn't come, only a suffocating feeling that the whole world, and even my man, was falling on top of my head. I'd become Esther Greenwood, the main character in Sylvia Plath's only novel. A bell jar was descending on me, and I had no idea how to stop it.

Chapter Five

I trailed behind Francis to the Camry and sat so far away from him my shoulder touched the door. We drove away in silence. I tried not to think about the fact that I was going insane, but the idea kept bobbing up into my consciousness. *Oh God,* I silently prayed, *please protect me.* The first verse of Psalm 27, one of my favorite Bible passages, came to me:

> *The Lord is my light and my salvation; whom shall I fear? The Lord is the stronghold of my life; of whom shall I be afraid?*

Rain glazed the ground. I focused on the dreamy names off the street signs to occupy my mind: "Chartres, Dauphine, Marais." They all sounded so pretty.

We should be enjoying ourselves tonight, I thought. *Instead he's nursing me while I have a nervous breakdown. How long is he gonna stick around if he thinks I'm a psycho?*

I hoped not too long. I knew how hard it was to deal with my mother, and I loved him too much to wish that kind of life on him.

Put my mind right fast, Lord. It's getting kinda hectic in here.

We pulled up in front of a line of old Greek Revival row houses.

"We're here," Francis said.

"Where?"

It wasn't Mama's address, although the row of houses looked like residences. For a second I thought he might be dumping my crazy behind on some of his friends.

"It's a bed and breakfast."

He took our bags out of the car and headed toward the corner house. I grabbed my purse and backpack and shadowed him.

The looming pastel building—so Parisian looking—could have stirred romantic fantasies in someone who was not seeing ghosts. Dark shutters bordered French windows, making a sharp contrast to the blush-colored brick exterior. Expansive second story *gul-rays* stretched across the length of the building. Francis knocked on the door, and a woman stepped outside and greeted him with a hug.

"*Coozine!*" she squealed.

Man, was she ever pretty: middle-aged, with thick, coarse hair plaited into twists. Her flawless skin was the color of dark chocolate, and her laugh was just as bittersweet, full of the wisdom of living long enough to know the good and evil of life.

"*Bienvenu, mon cher!*" she said to Francis when she released him.

"*Mèsi, tante.*"

The woman turned to me. "*Bonswa, gul!* Welcome to Baptiste Row Bed and Breakfast. I'm Marie. Ya must be Emme." The sounds coming out of her mouth dipped and ascended, as complex as a jazz melody.

"*Bonswa*, Miss Marie." I forced out a smile to return her generous one before shooting a look at Francis. "I just repeated what she said."

"Oh, I'm sure you'll be speaking Creole in no time."

When I frowned at his sarcasm he softened his edge. "Sorry. *Bonswa* means good evening."

"What does *tante* mean?" I asked Miss Marie.

"Auntie," Francis answered, his voice terse.

Miss Marie smirked, obviously aware of the tension between us, but Francis ignored her bemusement. "*Tante* and I are good friends. She calls me *coozine*—cousin, though I'm no more her cousin than she is my aunt. I stay here as often as she lets me." He chuckled. "Sometimes she don't let me."

"Mosta da time you don't make no reservation!" She wagged a finger at him before placing her hand on her ample hip. Now she looked at me, "Da boy pleaded for a room, poor little thing."

Francis nodded. "Yeah, 'poor little thing' is right after what you charged me."

"Ya betta be glad it's Thursday, 'steada Friday night."

I could hardly pay attention to their banter. I just wanted to lie down. But I did notice something different. She'd said "a" room, as in singular. That was a no-no to Francesco. Last night I lay alone in my Motel 6 digs. He must have been responding to my strangeness, but I was glad about it.

"*Mèsi*," I said to him. "That's gotta mean thanks. Right?"

He gave me a shy smile. "It does. *Dèriyin, mon choux.*"

I tilted my head, "What'd you say?"

His smoldering golden eyes swept over me. "I said, 'You're welcome, my sweet.'"

Miss Marie added, "Or he mighta called ya a cabbage." She laughed so hard she had to wipe her eyes on her apron. "Let's getcha upstairs. Gwan' be some puttin' it right tonight."

OMGosh! I thought, my face burning. *Does she think we're gonna . . . Lord, have mercy!* Miss Marie just laughed and waved away my chagrin.

The three of us swept up the dark wood staircase. Our hostess regaled us with tales about her great-grandfather, Joseph Baptiste. The devilishly handsome rogue had acquired the building by dubious means in the late 1800s. He had grandiose visions of what he'd do with the property, but alas, possessed too many vices. He ended up gambling the building away five years later. But Baptiste mourned its loss, and the could-have-been thriving Baptiste Row consumed him until he died.

Miss Marie had prepared the only one of the three rooms that had two beds in it for us: the "slave quarters." It was *literally* the slave quarters back in the day, but she'd made the tiny space utterly beguiling. The room felt cozy rather than cramped. I'd been on an emotional roller coaster, and the attic loft, with its painted white brick walls, cathedral ceilings, and skylight, was a welcome remedy for my indigo blues.

"It's amazing, Miss Marie."

"*Mèsi bien, ma chérie. Bon nuit!*"

With that she left us.

A pair of twin beds, with antique brass headboards, flanked a small bureau against the wall. It was easy to imagine a couple of mischievous kids, awake past their bedtime, exchanging whispers between beds. A narrow chest of drawers stood in the corner. Beyond it a fireplace warmed the room, its glowing flames softening the shadows.

The bedroom was attached to a sitting room, with an oak sleigh daybed, a rattan chair, and pieces of folk and outsider art to enliven the place. My favorite: a crazy-looking ship in a bottle thing, with a whole Crucifixion scene rendered inside.

I laughed out loud when I saw it. "Dude! A crucifix in a bottle! This is the *shiz.*"

He set our bags in the corner. "It's insane. I'm getting you one. I might even have to pay *Tante* for that one."

The bed called out to me, and I bounced on it to feel the firmness of the mattress. If there was any happiness to be found in my rotten mood, being there with him should have been it. He'd given me what he knew I needed, but tension still stood between us.

"Francis, I know you don't like this sort of thing. I just don't want to be alone tonight."

He avoided my gaze for a moment, which meant something difficult to hear was coming. I braced myself.

"Emme, you licked my neck. And that kiss? Baby, you did things to a brotha's mind and body you don't even want to know about."

"I'm sorry. I didn't mean to wake up anything that's s'posed to be asleep."

"What you think you awakened out there has been up and roaming about like a beast since I met you."

I lay back on the bed, already exhausted by the conversation. "What do you want me to say?"

He sighed. "I don't want you to say anything, but being aware of what you do to me would be helpful."

"I'll work on that."

"May I tell you a story?"

I wasn't particularly down with storytelling time, but if he was willing to make such a chastity-straining sacrifice for me, the least I could do was listen.

I turned my head to face him, and he leaned toward my bed, his hands on his thighs. "Once, a ridiculously seductive woman, probably as alluring as you are, asked Saint Francis of Assisi to share her bed. He surprised his fellow friars by saying yes."

I raised an eyebrow. Saint Francis was all about poverty, chastity, and obedience. Dude used to roll in the snow, naked, when his urges got out of control.

Francis continued. "He went to her room with her, and they closed the door behind them. They were alone, like we are, and it must have been pretty sweet in there, with the fireplace in the corner, reminiscent of the one behind you. The woman, who had one thing on her mind, crawled into bed and asked him to join her."

"What did he do?"

"He went to the fireplace first and climbed inside until flames engulfed him. From the fire he told her, 'I will come to you, but first you must join me in this bed of roses.'"

The two of us laughed, breaking some of the tension between us.

"Duuuuude, that's a wild story," I said.

Francis nodded, excited. "I know, right? Saint Francis was a man, but he was honorable. When he stood in that fiery furnace he showed the woman there was greater love than—you know—doing the do. As a result he converted her, but that wouldn't have happened if he hadn't gone with her in the first place."

I sat up and faced him. I wanted him to know I was hearing him, and not just with my ears.

"How can I make this easier for you?"

"By paying attention. Think about me and what I'm feeling. I want to give you the support you need, but you can't lose sight of me standing in the fire. This right here, being alone in a room with you after that move you put on me in the parking lot? That's my bed of roses."

"I don't want you to be uncomfortable."

"But I am uncomfortable, and a little worried. Not just about my own feelings. Physical intimacy, even a kiss, sometimes confuses you. And then you jet. Emme, you've left a brother hangin' for a lot less than this."

"That was then."

"In some ways, but we're complicated, Emme. We always have been. I don't want to lose you because I've got a temptation thing going on."

Before I could respond, the bloody visage of the deal girl popped up behind Francis. Like I needed to deal with her, too!

"What the heck do you want?"

Francis stumbled over words. "Wha . . . I—I just want to be with you without doing us any damage."

If I wasn't weary to the depths of my soul I'd have thought the situation was hilarious. The girl disappeared again.

I flung myself back down. "I want to be with you too, *papé*, but I'm exhausted. It's just one night. We'll be all right."

Francis frowned. He scanned the room, his mouth pressed into a grim flat line. "You weren't asking *me* what I want, were you?"

"Who else would I have asked?"

"What is this I'm feeling, Emme? It's sorta dark and sad."

"Heck if I know, Francis. Hey, will you keep the night watch with me? Please?"

"You know I will," he said, before he went into the sitting room, breviary in hand.

I was a little disappointed that he had promptly gotten up and left, but I knew he was spending some much-needed time alone with God. Soon enough the flames would engulf him in a way I didn't give enough respect to. A brotha was working hard to keep his honor and mine, and I blessed him for that. Like Tupac said, *I ain't mad at cha.*

Chapter Six

The dead girl showed up as soon as Francis went into the sitting room to pray. I'd edged toward the mirror to examine the toll the sucky day had taken on me, and there she was, right behind me like we were in a scene from a low-budget horror film. I'm the black chick. I was so getting killed early on, but I wasn't going without a fight, or at least some interesting characterization or comic relief.

"All right you creepy cow, what d'ya want now?"

She wanted a hug, apparently, because she wrapped

her arms around me. Her loose head lolled back, falling against her back with a sickening *thwok*.

Awwwwww, man! That was a bit much, even for Emme Vaughn. So many circuits in my brain blew I couldn't even scream.

She squeezed me like a pair of vise grips. Her form felt as solid as steel. Then, *whoosh!* The fullness of her grief slammed into me with such force it knocked a sistah on the ground.

Francis found me curled up in a fetal position. A soon as he touched me I squalled. Her losses broke the levee protecting my fragile emotions. Now I owned *her* flood of regrets. Her unlived life became my private hell.

Before she died the girl had been beaten; each blow wracked my body. The searing pain of her head being partially dismembered circled my throat. My entire body felt raw, like a throbbing wound before the intensity of the pain faded to an icy, black nothingness, along with my consciousness.

I hadn't fainted. Something supernatural happened. I knew I wasn't dead but trapped in a weird, psychic purgatory. I don't know how long I stayed in that state. It could have been seconds, hours, or days, before the darkness gave way to a blistering nightmare.

I dreamed I was inside a church filled with smelly

trash. A sheep lay on an enormous altar, already sacrificed. Two candles bordered its body, one burning bright, the other smoldering. The sheep's blood spread across the wood surface and drained to the ground in sticky pools. As I watched, its fleece turned to bare human flesh. Bizarre symbols rose as angry welts on its pale skin.

A choir of voices sounded, a macabre mockery of Gregorian chant. I opened my mouth to pray, but the words skipped like a broken CD. "Our Father . . . our Father . . . our Father . . ." The shadowy figure of a man stole behind me. Fear seized me, and I awoke with "our Father" still on my lips. As fast as I could I finished the prayer: *Whoartinheavenhallowedbethynamethykingdomcomethywillbedoneonearthasitisinheavengiveusthisdayourdailybreadandforgiveusourtresspassesasweforgivethosewhotrespassagainstusandleadusnotintotemptation.*" I took a deep breath. *"But deliver us from evil."*

Instinctively I touched the strange markings on my heaving chest. They had appeared mysteriously a few months ago, after Asmodeus, a powerful demon, attacked me.

I made the sign of the cross. "In the name of the Father, and the Son, and the Holy Spirit, Saint Michael the Archangel, defend us in battle. Be our protection against the wickedness and snares of the devil. May God rebuke him, we humbly pray, and do thou, O Prince of the heavenly host, by the divine power of God, cast into hell, Satan, and all the evil spirits who roam throughout the world, seeking the ruin of souls."

I called his name. "Saint Michael, are you there?" But I didn't feel or see a thing.

The archangel once told me my marks were a seal from God. Remembering this, my heart began to quiet. But I missed Saint Michael, who I sometimes called Brother, and wished he'd give me a sign that he was around. None came. The dream still disoriented me. My gaze bounced around the room until it fixed on Francis fast asleep in the other bed.

"Francesco?"

He didn't move.

Once again, I looked around the room. The charming décor no longer consoled me. I considered watching television to chase the silence away, but I'd seen enough disturbing images in that wretched dream. Instead, I closed my eyes.

Just listen, Emme.

The heater whirred. An appliance's hum droned on. Francis breathed deeply, heavy in slumber. Rain pattered outside, and the shower's mournful thrum recalled the dead to me.

Was that me lying on the altar? Was the dream a

premonition of my own murder? And who was the dead girl haunting me?

What's her name? I wondered. Was her mama inconsolable? Did her father vow to avenge her death? I wondered if her *beau* was as sleepless as I was, their tragic love story playing in his head? And why did she have so many regrets? She was young, maybe only Francis's age. No answers came to me; she remained as baffling as she was when she first appeared.

I hadn't intended to make this about me, but experiencing her death made me ponder my own pathetic life. I didn't have to look at myself long before I found Emme Vaughn sorely lacking. Lord, have mercy.

I was so stinkin' ungrateful. I knew how to say "please" and "thank you," but that wasn't wholehearted gratitude. And God help me, I didn't drink life in, savor it, and let it saturate my arid existence. Emme Vaughn had to change. Fast.

The sound of rain outside drew me to the balcony, and I stepped outside in my nightclothes into the frigid morning.

"Wooooot!"

The cold rain dappled my skin with goose bumps. It was freezing out there, but I felt alive.

Water streamed off my pajamas and snapped my colorless hair back into ringlets, but I wasn't worried about my coiffure. The hallowed rain had become a sacrament, baptizing me in thanksgiving. I tipped back inside the room, shivering in waves, my teeth chattering so loud they could have awakened Francis.

But I was *alive*!

Determination swelled in me. Sistah girl was gonna stop taking so much and start giving, even from my meager resources. "I do not possess silver and gold, but what I do have I give to you."

At the sound of my voice, Francis stirred.

I stood my full five feet and eleven inches, so full of faith it felt like my soul was touching heaven. Francis shifted his lanky frame on his bed, and in that moment I loved him as I never had before.

I padded to the corner and grabbed my duffel bag, laughing softly as I went. This occasion called for my cutest outfit, the scarf dress Francis had bought me when we first met. I dug it out of my bag, along with a shrug I borrowed from my girl Kosha. I was gonna rock Francis's world!

The heavenly smell of coffee and beignets captured my attention. Miss Marie must have been doing her thing in the kitchen. I tiptoed past my man to the bathroom to peel off my wet clothes and make myself gorgeous before he woke up. Twenty minutes later I came out as shiny as a new penny, which made me think of Penny Pop, Francis's former housekeeper.

I could almost hear her voice saying, "Chile, we some fine black womens!" I did her proud that morning, although if she were there she'd have flatironed my hair before I could say "happy I'm nappy."

Quietly, I made my way to the sitting room to lounge by the fireplace, cradling the worn prayer book I'd inherited from Jane Doe. I prayed the morning office, interceding for Francis, my mama, and the dead girl. Still deeply appreciative, I offered God some poetic praise in my composition book:

Friday morning, December 12, New Orleans
Baptiste Row B&B,
Francesco asleep in the next room.

Rain.

No Words

Today I stood outside.
The sky was a womb
And the Great Gray God
My Mother.

Her damp, silver
Fingers touched
All my exposed
Parts.

I think
I felt her Laughter.
Or maybe, She was crying.
I'm never sure of this.

I only know water,
The smell of wet earth,
And freshly bathed green
Scented Her dark body.

God's watery voice said
Nothing in particular;

Her aqueous,
Saturating voice
Spoke

Saying
No words
At all.

Renewed by grace, I got ready to serve. If Miss Marie would allow it, my man was getting breakfast in bed.

Before I headed downstairs I noticed a copy of the *Times-Picayune* newspaper on the floor. Impulsively I picked it up.

Hellooooo, dead girl. My friendly ghost's portrait smiled at me from the front page. Above her glamor shot a headline screamed "Tremé Residents Demand Justice in Girl's Murder."

I folded the paper closed and tossed it into the sitting room, using all the restraint I could muster. The dead would have to wait. I had a *living* man to take care of, and so help me God, I was going to be good to him.

Chapter Seven

Miss Marie had a feast spread out in the dining room. The table almost buckled under the weight of stacks of banana and praline pancakes, fresh fruit, scrambled, boiled, and deviled eggs with caviar, shrimp and grits with red-eye gravy, and paper-thin slices of smoked salmon. If you weren't a seafood lover, she had bacon and sausage links, patties, and fat broiled andouille. I nearly swooned, but I was on a mission, and followed the sound of music into the kitchen.

Miss Marie was spooning a beignet out of hot grease. The sweet aroma curled my toes in my diva boots.

"*Bonjou*, Emme. *Konmen lé'zaffaires?*" Miss Marie asked. "How're things?"

"How do you say, 'I'm doing good'?"

"Eh, make it easy on ya' self and say, '*C'est all right.*'"

"I'll make it easier still and say, 'I'm all right.'"

Her boisterous laugh filled the room before fading. "Sit a spell, Emme. There's a plate with ya name on it." Miss Marie gestured toward the breakfast nook. Like the rest of the house, the kitchen was beyond fabulous: antiques, art, food, and the radio playing some vintage New Orleans funk—The Meters, *They All Ask'd for You.* I swung my bottom to the beat until I sat it down on a stool, just as happy as I could be.

While I grooved and my stomach growled, Miss Marie wiped powdered sugar off her hands onto her apron and turned her compassion-filled eyes on me. "I don't mean to be nosy, and ya can tell me to mind my business, but Frankie, he's my *coozine.* I heard ya crying all night, *cher.*" Her shortened version of *chérie* sounded like "sha." I liked it.

"There's a lot going on with me, but I'm better now."

"Well, I didn't want to see ya gone 'fore I had the chance to ask."

My reply went missing as I gazed with longing at the fluffy pillows of fried dough in front of me. "Oh, man. Those smell so good, Miss Marie."

Her laughter rang out. "Help ya self, gul! Ain't g'wan be no starving to death in my *kwizin*." Which was the coolest way to say "kitchen" ever.

Before I started stuffing beignets in my mouth I got back to my mission. "Miss Marie, may I please take Franci—I mean Frankie his breakfast? I want to serve him in bed."

My face heated with embarrassment. "What I mean is I want to give him his food in the room. I won't be in bed *with* him. I didn't sleep with him last night either. I've never slept with anybody. I mean . . . you know . . . *slept* with them."

That laugh of hers filled the kitchen, but she grabbed an absolutely divine antique silver platter out of one of her cabinets. "No skin off my back, *mon chou*."

I wasn't sure if that meant she didn't think we were lovers or if she did, but it didn't matter. As happy as I felt, I was beginning not to care. Anyway, if our reps were already shot, there wasn't much we could do about it.

If a plate had my name on it, two had Francis's. I

loaded them up and added a tall glass of orange juice and a cup of coffee, just like he likes it, to the tray. Before I shuffled away with my abundance, I heaped a couple of eggs and some smoked salmon on the overburdened plates so he'd have a few sources of protein.

When I opened the door to our room, Francis charged out of the bathroom like a wild animal.

"Where have you been?" he demanded. A prominent vein in his neck stuck out like it'd pop.

I held up the breakfast tray. "Dude, chill! I wanted to do something nice for you."

We stood there for a few tense moments until Francis let out a breath I don't think he knew he was holding. He slumped onto the bed and cradled his head in his hands. "Girl, I thought you left me again."

I put the tray down and touched his knee. "The only place I was going was to get you some breakfast. I'd like to serve you in bed. So could you please sit back and let me do my thing?"

Francis stared at me like I was an angelic visitor, a silly smile plastered on his face. "You're really still here?"

"Boy, stop gaping at me and eat. I spent the last hour cooking those pancakes and pralines. From scratch." I winked at him.

While Francis busied himself with eating, I grabbed a beignet—it was still warm. Mercy! That was good eating! I picked up the newspaper, trying hard to look nonchalant.

Okay, dead missy, I thought, *you have my attention.*

According to the article, her name was Celestine Nuit, a name that conjured an inky night sky freckled with white stars. She was seventeen at the time of her demise two weeks ago, an orphan who'd never been adopted. Celestine lived in a home for girls, run by Poor Clares. I wondered if the Clare thing was fortuitous, since I was Chiara. If my patron saint had prayed her my way, I thought I could accept the madness a little better. A little.

Despite numerous hardships, Celestine was well on her way to being the star her name hinted at. She loved to act, sing, and dance and was accomplished at all three. I scanned the headline again: "Tremé Residents Demand Justice." Of course her community would be outraged.

"Where's Tremé, Francesco?"

He answered between pancake bites: "You're in it."

"Seriously?"

"*Mmmph.* You sure you don't want some of these? They're fantastic."

"Those are for you, *papé.* So, what's it like here?"

"Well parts of it are the straight up hood. You know the dude who created *The Wire* for HBO? He did a show about Tremé, too."

"So, it's an *interesting* community, like Baltimore?"

"Interesting is not the word, poet-girl. Tremé sizzles! The jazz is smokin' hot!" He swung his fork like it was a conductor's baton. "Crazy! Funky! Nasty jazz! They even have jazz funerals!"

"I'm going to have a jazz funeral if you keep wielding your fork like that."

But he was absolutely smitten. "And the brass bands, Emme! The brass bands!" Francis shuddered as if the thought of brass bands brought him more joy than he could stand.

"Tremé is a hotbed of African-American and Creole culture," he explained. "Musicians, poets, artists, businesspeople, activists, you name it, if they're cool, they live here. It reminds me of Harlem, only it's completely different. Ya know?"

"Not really." I tried to keep my voice even as I flashed him the paper. "This girl was murdered here."

"Let me see that." I could tell his antennae was picking up trouble signals as I handed him the paper.

"They don't know who did it," I said.

He scrutinized the paper. "That's messed up."

I hoped the next question I tossed at him would

sound casual." "So, what do you know about seeing the dead?"

He blinked and frowned, a bad combination. "Why do you ask, *mon amour chéri*?"

"We haven't talked much about seeing ghosts."

"Not for lack of me trying, Emme. You were a lot more mums-the-word about that than about seeing demons."

"But enough about me." I took the paper back, studied her face, and tried again. "What do *you* know?"

Thank goodness the man couldn't resist teaching me. He sat up on the edge of his bed so he was closer to me.

"'Haints' are what they call ghosts here," he said, "or should I say ghosts and apparitions, since there's a difference between the two."

"You had me at haints. What's the difference?"

"Ghosts are sorta insubstantial."

"You mean wispy? Sorrowful looking? Sometimes horrifying, especially when they show up like they did when they were murdered?"

"*Noooooo.*" He eyed me like he couldn't figure out whether he should continue or pelt me with questions. "What I mean is that ghosts don't take on a form that you'd identify as human. You might see them as orbs, or shadows. People into the paranormal believe it takes a lot of energy for a spirit to manifest as human. I mean, like, physical energy."

"Clarify 'physical energy' for me."

He pushed the breakfast tray aside. "Here's an example: a lot of times, a person will see a ghost or apparition when it's raining. That's because—"

"What about snowing? Could you see them on a day like yesterday when there were snow flurries mixed with rain?" I remembered that Father Miguel had appeared to me during a rain storm.

"Emme, you probably could see them on a sunny day without a hint of wind. An interesting aside: all over the South there's this shade of blue people are nuts about. It's called haint—or haunt—blue. Its roots are in the traditions African slaves brought to the New World. They painted their entrances and window openings haint blue because it symbolized the color of water. The slaves believed evil spirits, ghosts, and other demonic nuisances couldn't cross the water. You'll even find porches around here painted that color for protection."

"We can't paint our whole house that color when we get married, but what I'm getting at is what do *you* think about ghosts, Francis? Personally, and as a Christian?"

"In some of the Protestant deliverance ministries I've worked with, a common perspective was that all ghosts are evil spirits trying to pass themselves off as the dead."

"That's what I was taught, and since I saw demons at such a young age, whenever the dead popped up I'd rebuke them like I would a demon."

"Did that make them go away?"

"Yeah, but that doesn't mean what I did made them leave. They never seemed to hang around long anyway."

"From a Catholic perspective, there's nothing in the catechism about ghosts, which seems pretty smart to me."

"Why do you say that?"

"I think the less written about it in the catechism itself, the less people are encouraged to think about, or dabble in something so dangerous and unpredictable." He leaned forward and scrutinized me. Suddenly the space between the beds seemed way too small. I felt like a kid who'd gotten busted doing something I had no business doing.

His penetrating stare bore into me. "Have you been seeing ghosts?"

"You didn't answer my question, Francis. What do *you* believe?"

For a moment he paused. "I guess I *don't* believe

ghosts are always evil sprits. I mean, I know demons are all about deception, but I've read some convincing reports of rock-steady Christians seeing ghosts. And what about a few hard-to-come-to-terms-with passages in the Bible? Remember the story about the rich man and Lazarus? He wanted to go back to warn his brothers to check themselves before they wrecked themselves. How would he have gone back? It's possible that he thought he could visit them as a ghost or apparition. And don't forget the Transfiguration. Long-dead Moses and Elijah, hanging out with Jesus. Matthew 27:52–53 says just after the resurrection the tombs were opened and the dead walked around Jerusalem."

"Dude, don't make me think about zombies in the Bible."

"The risen Christ isn't a zombie. They probably weren't either."

"Good point, but let's get back to seeing the dead. So you think, biblically, there's some *loose* precedent for it?"

"Loose is right, because both the Transfiguration and the post-Resurrection dead stroll are mysteries. And here's another consideration: the Bible strictly forbids contacting the dead."

Francis pulled out his iPhone and went to Google. A few minutes later he had chapters and verses.

"Deuteronomy 18:10–12 tells us not to use mediums to speak to the dead or channel them ourselves, and 22:6–7 equates doing so to prostitution."

"What does wanting to hear from the dead have to do with hookin'?"

"I don't know. Maybe it's a matter of fidelity. If you're seeking the dead, you're likely doing so for a reason. Maybe you want assurance they're all right, or something altogether different that's not so benign, which sorta points to the fact that you should be seeking God and trusting him with the details of your life."

"That makes sense."

Francis picked up a beignet. Before he took a bite he clarified his position. "I'm not trying to take away from the importance of being faithful to God, but I think contacting the dead is a big no-no mostly for the same reason that everyone shouldn't be involved in casting out demons. If you open yourself to the spirit world, you're vulnerable to attack, deception, or a wicked combination of both. So, my Protestant friends in deliverance ministries have a point; I just wouldn't want to throw the baby out with the bathwater, or the dead with the demons."

"If you saw some of the stuff I have, you'd want to throw all that junk out."

"I don't doubt that I would, Chiara."

I sat back on the bed and took another look at Celeste's picture. "Why do you think they appear to people?"

"Maybe God gives people a few fleeting moments with their departed loved ones to comfort and encourage them. In those instances it could be a gift of grace. Other times the dead appear because a soul has some unfinished business to take care of. You and I believe in that place the Bible talked about where the rich man and Lazarus were. Sacred scripture calls it *sheol*, the place of the dead. We Catholics call it purgatory. Lazarus was rewarded in paradise, but the rich man had to cook a little longer in God's purifying oven. I think some ghosts aren't finished with something enough to go to purgatory yet. So they stick around and annoy people, or enlist their help. Of course, I'm no expert on that. Father Miguel wasn't big on talking about that kind of thing."

"What kinds of things do you think they want help with?"

He took another bite from his pastry and savored it before he answered. "It could be anything. Once, I saw a television show about a ghost who helped his relatives find a hidden stash of money."

"Must be nice."

"Paranormal circles cite plenty of cases where the deceased help solve his or her own murder."

"I never bought into that stuff. Those TV psychics seem so fake."

"Most of what you saw probably was. Not much reality in reality television. But some people, as you know, really do have incredible gifts. There's this old chick—she lives around here as a matter of fact. Her name is Mary Brooks. She's a very devout Christian. She's blind, but she can see what most folks don't wanna see. She works with the police sometimes and God uses her. She doesn't exploit her abilities either, and she's brought closure to some families who were really suffering."

Then why isn't Celestine harassing her, I thought. Which also begged the question: "Francis, do you think a human spirit can possess a person the way demons do?"

He thought for a moment. "No, I don't see how that could happen, but the scripture in Deuteronomy does forbid channeling. How that works, I'm not sure. I think a person who is a sensitive can empathize, even with the departed, to the degree that they feel another person's suffering deeply."

I set the newspaper down on the bed and looked into his face. "Has that ever happened to you?"

"I've had some painful experiences with my gift, but nothing ever happened that made me think a human spirit was trying to possess me. I might have felt a lot of their burden, but that's about as serious as it got." He eyed me with a smirk on his face. "So, is the girl on the front page the haint you've been vibing with?"

"Dude," I said, a little too loudly. "What makes you think *that*?"

"You are so not a good prevaricator, Emme. Is she the reason you cried all night? Please tell me yes, so I won't think it was because of me."

"I've got a lot going on. That's all."

"Yeah, you're finally seeing your mom today, and a dead girl is tormenting you. I'd say that's a lot."

"I never said a dead girl was tormenting me. Why can't this just be a discussion?"

"Why can't you answer a simple question? Is Celestine Nuit haunting you?"

I didn't answer, just stared back at him. His eyes told me he wouldn't pressure me. That's one thing I loved about Francis, his honest, oh-so-readable eyes. He set the breakfast tray on the chest of drawers and grabbed his breviary and my hand. "I think our 'discussion'"—he crooked his fingers on one hand into quote marks—"is something we need pray about."

In the sitting room we stood facing east while he made quick work out of praying the Office and asking for God's mercy and guidance. Sweet Francesco, he even prayed that God would give Celestine rest. Finally, we gave thanks and said, "Amen."

I knew what was coming next, and it wasn't another talk about seeing the dead. I had a person very much alive to attend to.

Francis's gentle eyes regarded me. "Ready to go see your *madre*?"

"As ready as I'll ever be."

My fiancé took my hand. I may have been about to walk into the unknown, but I'd do so with the very best person I knew. Somehow that made it all okay.

Chapter Eight

By the time Francis and I stepped outdoors into the gray-tinted day, the rain had slowed to barely a drizzle. It was "cold," although fifty-five degrees on a December afternoon in Michigan would have had folks unpacking their swimwear. Francis still hadn't broken out his heavy jacket, but he'd borrowed an umbrella from Miss Marie. I joined him beneath it, taking his hand.

"If you're trying to protect my hair, it's kinda late for that. I had a little worship-God-in-nature session this morning. This is as good as it'll get for me."

"Your hair is fine," he said, but I could tell he was a little agitated. "Do you feel like walking?"

I looked around as if Abigail Vaughn would jump out at me from behind a bush. "Does Mama live that close to here?"

"She's a few blocks away. That's one reason I tried so hard to get us a room at Miss Marie's."

The thought of being mere blocks from Mama made my heart slam against my rib cage. I placed my hand over my chest in a useless effort to still it, but a heady combination of wild excitement and awful trepidation wouldn't let me go. I tried to keep my expression as placid as still water, but I had a million questions.

"Does Mama live in 'sizzling' Tremé, or the straight up hood?"

He thought for a moment. "Her location would be the happy—or not so happy—medium, depending on whether she turns right or left when she walks out of her door."

We headed a few blocks northeast on Tremé to Esplanade and ambled past palm trees, groomed topiaries, and pastel dwellings with expansive upper- and lower-floor galleries. It was all so gorgeous, and this was Mama's neighborhood! Even if she lived in a tiny shotgun house nestled between the immense homes, she'd found a place of beauty to lay her head.

I thought of all the times we'd moved, and how she'd blacken the windows with paint whenever her paranoia went extreme. Just then the memory of her constant rambling, and making me hide in the dark so often, assaulted me, so much so I could almost smell the preternatural stench that used to emanate from her. My stomach lurched.

In those few blocks, my hope wrestled the negativity still clinging to me. Intellectually I knew the worst was over. Whoever she was now, she wasn't going to be the person I left in the mental hospital. Whether all that happened to us was my fault or not was moot. According to Jane Doe, Mama was neither schizophrenic nor possessed by demons. We'd start all over; we'd be all right.

"How far now?" I asked, more nervous than I'd ever been in my life.

"Just a few more minutes."

My inside felt abuzz again, which concerned me. I glanced around but saw no sign of Celestine, or anybody else who wasn't breathing.

"Wait," Francis said, stopping short. He zoomed in on me. "Do you see anything?"

"I see you, and this pretty neighborhood."

"No, nothing like that. I'm feeling something." He reached for me. "Take my hand."

I did, but his touch gave me no insight. The meshing of our gifts was far from an exact science. I could tell Francis was experiencing something deep. I just hoped it wasn't anything terrible.

"Just go with it, Francis, whatever it is."

We walked a little more than a block, then Francis pulled me behind him. "It's like a force is drawing me to this church." He pointed to a simple, white brick church.

"I hope the 'force' is the Holy Spirit."

"If it wasn't we'd be whooping on it right about now, Exorsistah."

Moments later we stood in front of St. Anna's Episcopal. It had a red door, which reminded me of St. Clare's in Detroit, only smaller.

"In the mood for a little liturgy?" I asked Francis.

He shook his head. "As appealing as that sounds, I don't think we're here for that. The question is, what are we here for?"

I didn't see any cars in the parking lot. What I did notice, however, was a big plastic sign on the front wall, partially shielded by a tree.

"Maybe that's what we're here for," I said, pointing to it. Zing! The tingling I felt buzzed up my spine all the way to the top of my head.

We walked up to the sign and stood in front of it, reading. The header on the sign was a rendering of Psalm 46:1: "God is our hope and strength, a very present help in trouble." Beneath the scripture were the words "Murder Victims." What followed was what looked like hundreds of names, genders, dates, and manners of death of NOLA's fallen.

"There are so many," I said.

Francis squeezed my hand, and his supernatural empathy flowed through me. Or was it my own? I couldn't tell when we were touching.

"It doesn't have to be supernatural," Francis said. "You'd have to be void of feeling not to be moved by this. I feel all this rage and sorrow. Their voices are crying out for justice."

I wondered if he heard Celestine's voice in that creepy chorus.

He knelt. "Here's Celestine Nuit's name on the bottom of the list. Do you notice something different?"

"Besides the fact that it's one of the newest ones?"

"Take a look at the whole sign, and then her name and manner of death."

I surveyed the list. Most of the victims were twenty-something males. Almost all of them had been shot. Sure, there were some female vics and guys in their thirties—even a few older men—but the violence in New Orleans seemed to be about the young. I'd bet good money most of those men were poor and black, caught up in the spiral of violence so prevalent for boys in the hood.

Celestine's stats stood out like glaring neon signs. "Her manner of death is listed as a homicide," I said.

"That's right."

"So what. She wasn't shot."

"Ah ha!" Francis exclaimed. "It doesn't say how she died at all. But you know what happened to her. Don't you, Emme."

"Maybe I'm assuming she wasn't shot because it didn't say so like most of the others."

"How did she die, Emme?"

"What do I look like, the medical examiner here?" I looked at the sign, wondering if my gut and God's guidance would tell me anything.

What am I missing, Lord?

But all I felt nudging me was the cold. Too darned cold for what the temperature was, even with the rain. The unmistakable weight of Celestine's hand pressed my shoulder.

Francis stood, frowning. "It feels preternaturally cold out here."

I tried my best to put on a poker face. "What do you want me to do?" I asked Celestine.

Francis answered. "It'd be good if you could tell

me what you see, and I feel. I'm just sayin'. This sign is working on a brotha. But take your time if you need to."

My haint didn't speak to me in words, but rather impressions. Two emerged at once: an almost déjà vu sense of the conversation I had with Francis, when he told me sometimes the dead appeared to enlist our help. The other was something like a vision, but I wasn't seeing it with my inner eye. I could feel rather than see it.

I know that sounds nuts, but it's what I experienced: a presence I believed was human. Dude must have been almost seven feet tall. He moved swift as a ninja behind me. An awful *chook* sound followed, then a white-hot burning at my neck, preceding the shock of knowing.

So my new friend didn't die instantly. And I felt every bit of the horror she did. I teetered until Francis caught me.

"Stop it!" I yelled at Celestine. "This is making me sick!"

Francis gathered me into his arms. "You aren't talking to me, are you?"

"Don't ask me any more questions, Francis. I can't answer them."

"It's okay. Let's get away from this thing. I know the temperature dropped because of something other than the weather." He searched my eyes. "It's her, isn't it?"

"I'm freezing, Francis. Can't that be enough?"

"I'll let this go. For now." He released me, and we walked toward Mama's place no more than two blocks from the church.

Turns out Mama's house was not luxurious with a gallery on both levels, nor was it a shotgun shack. She lived in a sunshine yellow Creole cottage duplex that seemed to smile at me. Unfortunately my nerves were shredded. Francis had to help me up the concrete porch steps, or I'd have stood on the sidewalk hyperventilating.

"You can do this," he urged. "She's gonna be so happy to see you."

Both front doors were those steel, security numbers so formidable I doubted if bullets could have penetrated them. Those big monsters stood in ridiculous contrast to the welcoming French doors most of her neighbors' houses had. Wrought-iron-barred storm doors safeguarded the front of Mama's doors, and I don't think she just dug the fancy lacework. Seeing that fortress hearkened back to our worst days. My stomach plunged down to my Prada boots.

"She's paranoid again, Francis. I can tell."

I wanted to bolt, but he'd taken hold of my arm when he helped me up the stairs, and he held me fast.

"*You* sound paranoid, baby. I told you this is a mixed neighborhood. It gets its share of crime. As you know, a girl just got killed around here. Maybe your mother wants to protect herself."

"Or maybe she's painted the windows black and is wearing aluminum foil on her head, talking about the CIA and aliens."

Francis pressed the doorbell. Voices sounded within her citadel. Then he knocked on a panel of glass between the iron on the storm door, a totally ineffective move.

"She's never going to hear that through ol' impenetrable."

He tried again, ignoring my remark.

"She probably don't want no visitors. Ask me how I know." Oh, man. I'd reverted back into ghetto speak. I always did that when I was scared or frustrated. If Mama did open the door soon, she'd find a wisecracking hood rat standing there.

Francis tried knocking one more time, then the muffled strains of a man's voice penetrated the steel.

"Who is it?"

"Who is *that*?" I said, louder than I intended to.

"My name is Francis Rivera. I'm looking for Ms. Abigail Vaughn. I have someone with me I'm sure she'll want to see."

"Francis? Dude!" I stage-whispered. "You don't be tellin' nobody your real name not since I've known you."

"I do today. Relax."

We waited the longest thirty seconds ever until the door cracked. I processed the brown eye with long, feminine lashes, complete with mascara, peeking at me as if in pixels. There was a mole just beneath where she'd put on eyeliner. Mama used to call it her beauty mark. In an instant the door swung open and her face filled in. A thousand emotions flooded my being. Fear fled, and so much gratitude overflowed from my heart I could hardly stand it.

"Mama," I choked.

"My baby!"

I flew into her arms and we cried all over each other right there on the porch, for a very, very long time.

Chapter Nine

The first thing Mama did after we finished snottin' and cryin' was stroke my kinky white hair. "How did you get it this color?"

"Only my stylist knows."

Her laugh sounded angelic. "Well, I like it," she said. "It reminds me of a friend of mine."

"It reminds me of a friend of mine, too." Jane Doe had the same lack of hair pigmentation and not because she was old.

Mama was still gorgeous, the most amazingly

good-looking creature I'd laid eyes on in forever. She'd replaced her broken teeth with implants that looked so natural, if I didn't know her original smile, I'd never have guessed. Her curly hair, very short now, haloed around her head in a cute 'fro. I couldn't stop staring at her.

She wasn't rail thin anymore. N'awlins eating must have been good to her. I squeezed her again, just because her fuller figure reminded me of when I very small and she was still soft and curvy, like mamas should be. I'd forgotten about the men watching us until the dude who'd come to the door first cleared his throat.

Mama wiped her eyes again and reached for his hand.

"Baby," she said, "this is my daughter, Emme."

If we were in a comedy, this would have been the part where the sappy music abruptly ended with the sound of a needle scratching a record. I'd never in all my eighteen years heard my mama refer to someone else as "baby." *I* was Abigail Vaughn's baby! Not some man.

"Baby" held out his hand for me to shake, but I stood there glowering until a nudge from Francis prompted me. I shook his hand. Hard.

"Firm handshake," he said with a chuckle. "I'm Jack. It's good to finally meet you."

I didn't say a word.

When he released my hand I noted the pinched expression on Mama's face. She had a dang-gone boyfriend, and she wanted me to like him! And here I thought Francis was going to be a problem.

I sized Jack up. He wasn't hard on the eyes: a pretty yellow man with Cab Calloway good looks. His voice, sans the heavy Creole accent, was smooth as radio jazz. I wondered if he traveled a lot, lived in a lot of places, or simply came from somewhere else.

I've had a lot of self-serving thoughts about Francis's gifts, but I'd never wished I had the full measure of his discernment more than at that moment. I could tell you about demons, or angels, and seeing the dead, but my mama's boyfriend was a complete and utter mystery.

Jack jumped right in. "And who is your young man, Em?"

"Excuse me?"

First of all, if anybody was going to ask me about Francis it should have been my mama. Second, nobody called me "Em" but her, doggone it!

I'd gotten good at talking smack to grown folks in my exile. I was so at the verge of letting somebody—most likely Jack—have it. But a squeeze on the shoulder from Francis kept my tongue.

Francis stepped to Jack. "I'm Francis Rivera, sir."

He didn't hesitate to shake Jack's hand. Nor did he look like he was trying to break his fingers. And why did he tell them his name was Francis? He didn't even let his godmother, Mother Nicole, call him that.

"I heard you say your name at the door," Jack said. "That's not what I'm asking, young man."

"I'm a musician, and I love Emme," he said. "I plan to marry her as soon as she'll have me."

My head turned to Mama fast enough to give me whiplash. She raised a perfectly manicured eyebrow. "Emme is only eighteen."

"Yes, ma'am, I know."

"And how old are you, Francis?"

"I'm twenty-one."

"I'm assuming you've been dating Emme long enough to ask for her hand. Does that mean that you, a grown man, was dating my underaged daughter?"

"No. Not at all. I waited until she turned eighteen."

"That sounds like something some kind of pervert would say."

All the red in him rushed to Francis's face. "Oh, no ma'am. I just respected Emme."

"You call sniffing around my underage daughter until she came of age, and three months after you started seeing her pressuring her into marrying you, for God only knows what reason, respect?"

She flummoxed him. "Uh . . . I . . . uh . . . planned on speaking to you privately, but Mr. Jack put a brotha on the spot."

"*Put a brotha on the spot?*" she repeated tightly, as if Francis had just spit a few lines from *The Chronic* album. She looked him up and down with an icy expression on her face. "Francis, who are your parents?"

He recovered the king's English quickly. "I'm sorry, Ms. Vaughn. I'm a little nervous. My mother raised me. Her name was Francesca Peace. Five years ago she died of breast cancer. After that I drifted for a few years, until I finally honored her deathbed request and went to meet my father. His name was Miguel Rivera. He was a priest. He died last week."

"You don't need to stand out here on the porch and recount your history, *baby,*" I said. "Jack didn't have to put all his business in the streets. I don't even know his surname."

"Our last name is Washington," Jack said, looking at me with a twinkle in his eyes.

"Our?"

"We can talk about everything inside, Emme," Mama said. "Please come in."

Francis's sob story seemed to soften her to him. "I'm very sorry for your losses, Francis."

"Thank you, Mrs. Washington."

Bing! That's when the lightbulb came on over my head.

She got married! I couldn't even say the words because the truth snatched the breath from my lungs. She never even dated back in the day.

How long had they been together? Surely she couldn't have been dating while possessed. Ms. Jane said it took her a full year to deliver Mama. Did she hook up with this dude as soon as she was free? The year I was hiding from the foster care system, when my friend Kiki and Jesus were the only protection I had, my mama was *courting*?

"We have some catching up to do," she said. "Please."

"Come on, Chiara," Francis said, tugging at my arm. "Everything will be okay."

But it didn't feel like everything was going to be okay. Life had gone all topsy-turvy. For all the fretting I'd done on the way in, I never considered the possibility that she'd be happily married.

Happily. The word stirred my guilt. How could I not want Mama to be happy? *I do want her to be happy. Don't I?*

Before I had time to get to the core of that burning question, I wandered into the parlor for surprise number two: Mama had a wall of horror worse than the murder victims sign outside of St. Anna's.

Newspaper clippings and crime scene photos of none other than Celestine Nuit in her pretty ballgown were mounted where family photos should have been. It was the kind of thing cops or crazy people did.

A wave of nausea seized me. All I could think was that mama was still sick and that dead heifer Celestine was trying to possess us both! Francis must have been wrong! We weren't sensitive. We were some kind of prey for a vindictive spirit.

I also wondered if those paranoid demons had taken Mama in their grip again. Luke 11:25, about people newly delivered from demonic possession, came to mind:

> When an unclean spirit goes out of someone it wanders through waterless country looking for a place to rest, and not finding one it says, "I will go back to the home I came from." But on arrival, finding it swept and tidied, it then goes off and brings seven other spirits more wicked than itself, and they go in and set up house there, and so that person ends up worse off than before.

Oh, Lord, I thought, *am I gonna have to exorcise my own mama?* But Jack seemed like a levelheaded man. Why would he even let her put such things up on the wall?

Francis guided me to the sofa, and I sat down, crestfallen. *Lord, you didn't bring me here after all I've been through only to find her sick again, did you?*

No! He wouldn't do a sistah like that. I had to get a grip.

Emme Vaughn, I said to myself, *you'd better do like Father Miguel and Saint Michael the Archangel taught you: watch and pray.*

Francis gestured toward the montage on the wall. "That's interesting."

"It's a project Jack and I are working on," Mama said.

"What kind of project?" Francis asked as casually as if he were talking about her knitting. Jack dismissed his question with a wave of his hand.

"I'm a private investigator. I have a personal interest in a local case the police aren't forthcoming about. I set up our own little task force here, but we don't want to get into that when we're getting to know one another."

My relief at hearing Jack was a PI was almost palpable. The truth is if he weren't my mama's husband, and my mind weren't totally blown by the notion of him period, I might have liked the man. But I couldn't focus on approving or disapproving of my stepfather now. Another couple of questions nagged me, one being why was a picture of the dead girl who was stalking me on my mama's wall? But the one that bothered me most was far more personal. If Mama was okay enough to get married, and it just so happens she married a private investigator . . . um . . . why in the heck-e-naw hadn't she looked for me?

Nobody in the old neighborhood mentioned they had seen her since she was institutionalized. The question churned inside of me, growing hotter and hotter until I felt like a cauldron of anger about to boil over.

Jack tried to dissipate some of the tension in the room. "I believe your mama prayed you here. How did you find us, Em?"

"Nobody calls me Em but my mama."

"Jane Doe gave us the address," Francis answered, his cheerful voice contrasting with my flat tone.

"*Jane Doe?*" Mama said. "How did you find *her*? She seldom leaves her hermitage."

"Probably the same way you found her."

Her reaction was so subtle I'd have thought I'd imagined it if I hadn't known her face so well. My insolence surprised her. I wasn't crazy about it either, but nastiness kept flying out of me.

I tried to soften my tone. "I went to St. Dymphna's to look for you, and one of the orderlies, Deandre Cooper, told me that you'd left two years ago with Miss Jane. I did a little detective work of my own after that and ended up at St. Benedict's Abbey. Father Don did the rest. Not that I deserved to know anything, since I left you in that horrible place."

"Oh, Em," she said. "That wasn't your fault."

Hello again, Sistah Salty! "Then whose fault was it? Yours? How could that be, Mama? How could being possessed be *your* fault?" I waited for her to be honest and say she was sorry she had been foolish enough to invite the demons into her like Ms. Jane said, but she stayed quiet.

Jack spoke up, "I understand this is difficult for you, Emme—"

"You don't understand *jack*, Mr. Washington, unless *your* mama was paranoid and crazy as all hell like mine."

My mama's mouth flew open. *"Emme!"*

"Why didn't you try to find me, Mama? And don't tell me you did. I was all up in the hood when Jamilla got possessed, and nobody had seen you."

She placed her hand over her heart. "Jamilla was possessed?"

"Jamilla?" Jamilla is fine! I think a better question is what about *Emme?* Remember her? Your daughter? The one who was pretty much on her own since the age of twelve? *I'm* the one who had to run away, again and again, to protect myself from stuff I don't

even want you to know about. I lived on the streets, Mama, squatting. You have no idea how many pimps and macks tried exploit a sistah, and I had to battle them all while warring with demons!

"*High school?* I missed it, and all the stuff that goes with it like homecoming dances and prom. I never had the chance to feel like the princess at the ball. Never walked across that stage with a diploma in hand. And you know what? I went through that mess alone, and the only thing that didn't make me lose my natural black mind was that I thought I'd find my way back to you and we'd be a family again. But you got started without me!"

I snatched my notebook out of my purse. "Look at this junk! I wrote it on the way here." I tossed my notebook on the coffee table. "Life for me ain't been no crystal stair, Mama! But apparently it's improved *a lot* for you. I can't believe how stupid I've been. How could you find a *husband* and not me?"

Jack picked up my notebook, but Mama just sat there with tears streaming down her cheeks. I turned my head and squeezed my eyes shut to keep my own tears from falling, hating myself. It felt as if my throat were on fire from the effort not to cry. Francis pulled me into his arms.

That was it. One tiny act of compassion was all the permission I needed to finally let the hurt I'd tried to keep so carefully locked within me free. I completely lost control, my body convulsing with sobs.

Francis stood and pulled me to my feet. "Is there somewhere I can take her?" he asked.

Mama said, "Let me talk to her."

"That not a good idea, Abby," Jack said. "Francis, you can take her to the first room on the left. It's our guest room."

They have a guest room, I thought. *To welcome people to their lovely Creole cottage, but I was homeless, and she didn't take the time to find me.* I managed to choke out the words, "It wasn't supposed to go like this!"

"It is what it is, baby," Francis said.

He led me to the guest room full of the cozy little touches I knew to be my mama's: a few good antiques, a little bit of art. I cried even harder. Lord, have mercy. It even had a quilt that looked pretty darned close to the pink one with the butterflies she'd made for me when I was little.

"This is crazy. Look at this place. It's better than how we lived when I was growing up."

"Your mother was sick when you were a kid."

I tried to pull myself together, hiccuping the words. "I know. I should be happy for her."

Francis held me. "You don't have to explain

anything to me. I knew how hard this would be. It's never exactly like you think it'll be. Sometimes it's better, and sometimes it's worse, but these weird reunions are always complicated."

"She has a new family."

"She has a husband, Emme. You found someone to love, too, in what you call your exile."

"But I wasn't looking for love when we met that night in Walgreens. The most I hoped for was that I wouldn't get tossed out in the street in the middle of the night."

He laughed. "Come on. You know you thought I was hot. You kept staring at me."

"I still wasn't looking for love. It just happened."

"Maybe theirs did, too."

"How could she move on without me?"

"We all move on, Emme. It's like you told me how you felt when you stood before that icon of St. Maria Goretti. You said it was as if she were saying to you, 'We tried.' That's all a person has sometimes. Right?"

"That's just it. She didn't try."

"For a reason, I'm sure."

Francis hadn't closed the bedroom door behind us, and I saw Mama and Jack looking in on us.

"Are you okay, baby?"

"Oh, now *I'm* baby again?"

I couldn't seem to keep myself from biting her head off. What was wrong with me?

Jack came up behind her and put his hand on her shoulder. "She's not ready yet, Abby. You've got to give her time."

She shuffled back into the parlor, but Jack lingered. His soothing voice poured over my raw emotions like olive oil on a wound. "You take all the time you need, Emme. That woman loves you. I *gua-ran-tee* it." He drew out the syllables to sound like exaggerated Cajun.

"My head hurts pretty bad," I said.

"Let me get you something for that," Jack said, before he left Francis and me again.

"Come on, X," my sweetheart said. "Lay down for a few." He took the butterfly quilt off the bed and waited until I kicked out of my diva boots before he helped me settle down.

"The butterfly is the symbol of a soul's metamorphosis," he said, "from grubby little caterpillar to flying beauty. You've crawled on your belly long enough, but that part of your life is over now. I know what you're feeling at the moment seems bizarre, dark, and disorienting, but it's only your chrysalis. You are so close to your change, Chiara. God is going to restore all that you lost. I just know it."

"I'll try to remember that, 'cause it sure doesn't feel like it."

He tucked me in. "Who says you have to feel it for it to be real?"

"Can you give me a little time alone?"

"Sure. I'll be in the parlor. Okay?"

I nodded. My temples throbbed in pain.

All I could do was hunker down, burrowing beneath the folds of pink covering me. If my change was near I was none the wiser. All I knew was that God had given me what I asked for. If only he would teach me what to do with it.

Chapter Ten

The headache medicine Jack gave me knocked me out. I don't know how long I slept, but when I woke up, it didn't feel like the end of the world anymore. Exile was overrated. My beautiful, sane, unpossessed mama was in da' house, and I wanted to go out where she was and just look at her. Francis was right. If we had survived all we did, we'd figure out the rest together. I'd told the Lord I was going to stop being so self-absorbed, and I intended to stay true to that promise.

"Sorry, Lord. That whole new husband and not looking for me thing threw me for a loop."

I flung the quilt off, but despite my bravado I still felt as fragile as glass. A peek in the mirror above the antique dresser confirmed what I suspected: I looked a steaming hot mess. I smoothed my white hair as best I could, stretched my long frame, and soldiered on into the parlor where Mama, Francis, Jack, and what mystery novels would call "a mysterious stranger" congregated.

I didn't know who he was, but bruh man was hot as fish grease! He was young, not much older than Francis, and oddly familiar. I had the most bizarre sense that I'd known him all my life, only I'd never laid eyes on him.

Mama saw me standing at the entrance to the parlor and called out, "Emme?" Her voice was reticent, like I'd made her afraid of me.

The men stood, and I noticed the stranger had basketball-star long legs. He was taller than six foot two Francesco. Mama would call him a tall drink of water.

I noticed he was dressed immaculately in elegant black slacks and a white dress shirt. He still had on a gray, striped tie, but it lay askew at his neck.

He was checkin' me out.

Francis came over and flung a protective arm

around me. He kissed me on the lips longer than he normally would in front of people. I had the distinct feeling he was marking his territory, but I had to love a brotha for letting it be known that I was off the market.

The atmosphere in the room grew cooler.

What's up with that? The words "watch" and "pray" impressed themselves on my spirit.

"Did you rest okay, *mon amour chéri?*" Francis said.

The stranger snorted at Francis talking like the natives.

"I slept as well as could be expected. What'd I miss?"

"You don't want to know."

I didn't bother to ask Francis what he meant. I felt the stranger's stare fixed on me, and my gaze flickered to him once again. Francis noticed, and his jaw tightened, so I tried to play it off. "Don't tell me; this is my new brother."

Mystery man took a few lengthy strides on those endless legs until he stood in front of me. He took my hand in his, and kissed it longer than good manners called for.

"I am Jean-Paul Darling. Darling is my surname. I'm not flirting with you." His voice dripped with honey.

"Do you have to announce that every time you say your name?"

"*Non*," he answered, never breaking eye contact. "Sometimes I *am* flirting."

Up close and personal he was even more beautiful than he was from a distance. His sculpted face looked as regal as a Benin bronze sculpture, and his luminous dark skin could have been awash in blackberry juice. Jack came over to us and gave him one of those manly claps on the shoulder. "Emme, Jean-Paul is like a son to me."

Jean-Paul agreed. "He's been my mentor since I was six years old. It was he who taught me to be a man."

Jack cleared his throat, as if Jean-Paul's praise made him uncomfortable. "Back then I was a cop," he said. "I'd have adopted him, but I wasn't married, and in my line of work, I wasn't the best candidate. But Jean-Paul needed me, and I made time for him. It was my way of giving back."

"My mother was murdered when I was five," Jean-Paul explained. "The psychiatrists said I had post-traumatic stress syndrome. The nuns at the orphanage said I was incorrigible until Jack came along." Now he really laid it on thick. "All I know is I was given a new life because of the kindness of this man."

Even after that gushing display I was still skeptical. I'd had a few foster fathers who I thought were all that before they violated me. I wasn't quite ready to sing Sister Sledge's "We Are Family."

"Come have a seat, Emme," Jack said. "Francis was just telling us about his music."

Not that anyone could get a word in about it the way Jean-Paul started chattering like a monkey about how close he was to my mama. Francis and I took the love seat, and Jean-Paul sat on an upholstered chair directly across from us.

"And you are her baby girl," he said. "Ah, the stories she has told me about you. I think she hopes we will make a . . . how do I phrase this? An *indelible* connection."

"If you want an indelible connection you should get rid of dial-up."

Francis stayed quiet, but I could see that dimple peeking at me. It had been seldom seen since I walked into Mama's house.

I figured some civility to my mama was in order after I'd gone off on her. Besides, I genuinely wanted to know about her new life.

"How long have you and Jack been married, Mama?"

Francis covered his mouth with his hand as if the gesture would shut me up.

Mama looked reticent, but tried to smile and give a cheery answer. "We got married on August twenty-ninth of this year."

"Wow," I said with more edge than I intended. "You got married three days before I went looking for you. If I'd have known you were on your honeymoon, I'd have skipped spending my birthday in a fleabag motel in Auburn Hills being attacked by demonic forces and heartbroken because I had no idea where you were. I hope you had a better time than I did."

Sister Salty was back. At least I didn't yell that time.

Mama sat up straighter. "I'd like to tell you how everything happened, if you'll allow me to."

"Go ahead, Mama. I'm still waters over here."

She clasped her hands together and laid them in her lap, and despite my appalling attitude I felt compassion well up inside me. She was still my mama. I'd missed her. She had asked demons to possess her to keep them from getting to me. It was crazy, but she loved me enough to try to spare me.

She took a deep breath and launched into her story. Some of the details were already familiar to me.

"After Jane checked me out of St. Dymphna's, it took her a full year to free me."

"She told me that."

"In that time I moved through the various stages of demonic infestation: from possession, to oppression, and finally to different degrees of freedom in Christ. Jane made it clear that I had been out of touch with reality for so long that I'd spend the second year learning how to live again. I had to relearn everything. A case manager was assigned to help me with the basics."

"She didn't teach you the basics of how to find your kid?"

"I thought you said you wanted to hear this."

"I do." I blew air from my cheeks, trying to release some of the rage I'd obviously buried within. "I'm sorry. Please finish."

"I didn't see the case manager for long. I started having nightmares, and knew I had to come here."

"For what?"

She hesitated. "I needed to find someone."

Jean-Paul chuckled. "Wait for it. Three . . . two . . . one . . ." When I didn't say anything he was clearly disappointed.

"That one was way too easy," I said. "She practically handed it to me on a platter."

Jack added, "Your mother came to me soon as she arrived, delicate as a little brown bird. I had to take care of her."

Everyone seemed to be waiting for me to say the

obvious: "If you went to a private detective first," blah, blah, blah. I took perverse pleasure in acting like I didn't notice.

"Who were you looking for?"

"No one you've ever met, Emme."

Interesting how she phrased that. No one I'd met, but perhaps this person was someone I'd heard about, especially since Jane Doe had filled in so many blanks about my history.

"Why are you looking into that girl's murder?"

Jack answered. "Tina was one of my kids, too. On Saturdays I'd take Jean-Paul to classes at a children's theater. She was one of the brightest, most talented kids in the bunch, and crazy about Jean-Paul. We ended up spending a lot of time with her. The girl kept her crush on him all her life."

So my dead friend got her acting chops at a local children's theater, the people who loved her called her Tina, and she had a love jones for the fine brotha sitting across from me. All this information humanized her for me, and the sadness that had swallowed me whole the night before opened its yawning mouth again. But I pushed it away with the sheer power of my need to know the truth.

"Tell me more about what happened after you got here."

"I sought out Jack's services because he offered

free consultations. I had very little money. He ended up hiring me to work for him while we searched for the person I was trying to find. That's how I met Celestine, through Jack. She was a sweet girl. I'm hoping some of the . . . *special skills* I still have can help."

I turned to Jack, completely ignoring the fact that she worked for a private detective and so should have been able to figure our how to find her own daughter. "So, you know about the . . . uh . . . *special skills* she's talking about? And just so we're clear, she doesn't mean typing and filing."

"I know about them, and about yours, too. And since you asked me a question, you should know I think you need to adjust your attitude."

"And I think you haven't earned the right to tell me what to do, and she forfeited hers, let's just say, for obvious reasons."

Francis rubbed his temples as if I'd given him a headache. But Jean-Paul regarded me with what appeared to be mild amusement.

"You don't play well with others, do you, Emme?"

"I'm an only child." I looked at my new stepfather. "So, Jack, our abilities don't seem unusual to you?"

"I've been in this city a long time, Emme. New Orleans is what the old folks call a thin place. The divine and the diabolical bump up against the ordinary, all day, every day."

"So I've heard."

Francis finally spoke. "What happened to Tina, Mr. Washington?"

"She went missing a few weeks ago," Jack said. "They found her in a field wearing a white party dress. Nobody could figure out where she got it, or why she had it on. She left home that afternoon in plain clothes and told the abbess she was going to the movies. Alone. Whoever murdered that poor kid beat her and cut her throat from ear to ear. Almost took her head off."

"I'm sorry for your loss, Mr. Washington," Francis said. "Forgive me if I sound insensitive asking this question, but did she have any risk factors? Something or someone in her life that would have put her in harm's way?"

Jean-Paul nearly spat the words. "She was a saint! A pious girl who never even kissed a boy!"

Saint? Maybe not if she was sweet on Jean-Paul and running after him from the time she was a kid. And who wouldn't want to kiss him? Besides me.

Jack answered Francis, "The police went over her life with a fine-tooth comb. Even Jean-Paul and I were suspects. But the murder rate keeps climbing, and her case became just another one in the pile."

"Assez!" Jean-Paul said with a frown. "This conversation is too heavy. How about a light repast? Who wants some wine? And a little bread and cheese?"

"That's sounds like a fine idea," Jack said.

"I'll have a glass," my mama chirped.

Jean-Paul stood on his endless legs, stretched, and regarded Francis and me.

"Yes, thank you," Francis said. I had never known him to take a drink of anything other than water and coffee. I didn't have long to ponder it, however. Jean-Paul was waiting for my answer. I had the distinct feeling he was testing me.

"I'm underage."

And there was that unsettling grin of his again. "But of course, Emme," he said, then repeated, "of course."

He never offered a substitute.

Chapter Eleven

What a lively bunch we were, the five of us around the coffee table making small talk while they sipped a Merlot and I nursed a glass of water and knocked off the Brie and French bread. Conversation had become a minefield, and none of us knew who'd misspeak next and set off an explosion.

Mama was brave enough to breach our momentary truce. "I forgot to ask you how Jane Doe is doing these days."

"She's dead." After I said it, I felt bad about not

putting that more delicately. "I'm sorry. She passed away about a week ago. But she wanted to be with Jesus. I'm sure she's happy. Like, *really* sure."

She laid her hand over her heart. "Jane Doe is gone?" She shook her head slowly. "Hard to believe. I thought the woman was invincible."

"She was!" I said, remembering my friend. "She left here on her own terms, probably giving Saint Peter directions about how he should open the pearly gates."

"That was Jane." Mama's downcast eyes indicated she had retreated into a memory. Whether it was a good or bad one, I didn't know.

"Jane is gone," she said, a statement this time rather than a question.

"I know, right? I had to talk myself into it, too," I said. "Every day something comes up I wish I could ask her about."

"Me, too," Mama said. "Especially today."

She sat her wine down on one of the coasters she'd carefully laid on the coffee table. This time she looked me full in the face. "I know you're terribly disappointed in me, Emme, and God knows I don't want to upset you any more than I have. But you should know that it was Jane who told me not to contact you."

I stammered before I could get my words out. "Ms. Jane told you that?"

"It's the truth, Emme."

"Would anybody else like to hurt me?" I screeched. "I'm nice and vulnerable now. You can get some good licks in."

Francis placed his hand over mine. "Nobody wants to hurt you. I'm sure if Ms. Jane told your mom that she had her reasons."

"Yeah, reasons. Everybody has 'em, and they can dredge 'em up for every godforsaken thing they do."

"Not every godforsaken thing," Jean-Paul said. "Sometimes things simply are what they are. They happened how they happened, and that is that."

"Who asked you?" I snapped.

He chuckled. I couldn't seem to ruffle him. Mama, on the other hand, was an easier target. She tried to explain herself again.

"I can't emphasize this enough. I was more like a child than an adult initially. When I said I had to learn how to do everything, I wasn't exaggerating. I didn't even know how to talk to people anymore."

"You must have known how to talk to Jack. Or did you two not bother with *talking*?"

As soon as it came out of my mouth I knew I'd said too much. Mama didn't shrink from my disrespect this time. "Perhaps *you* need to learn how to talk to people, Emme."

"And they're off!" Jean-Paul said. Francis covered his face with his hands.

Now Jack came at me. "I took care of your mother. I'm sure Francis takes care of you."

I don't honestly think he meant that in a bad way. Jean-Paul, however, found a way to taint a perfectly benign statement.

"I'm sure he takes care of her, too, Papa Jack."

"That's not helping, Jean-Paul," Jack said.

It wasn't, and I was about to open up a can of whoop butt on him when Francis defended my honor. "We happen to have a chaste relationship. Not that it's any of your business, Jean-Paul."

"A chaste rock star. How curious," Jean-Paul said.

"I'm a musician," Francis said tightly. "Not a rock star."

"I am proud of you, Francis," Jean-Paul said, his droll mockery evident. "You've managed to maintain your virginity in a business where women—I believe the popular term for them is groupies—readily offer themselves to anyone with a modicum of talent and a road crew. You are a virgin, correct?"

Francis wasn't quick to respond to that one.

Mama spoke up. "I'm curious about that myself."

After trying to make Jean-Paul burst into flame

with my eyes, I attempted a diversion. "Mama, I'm a virgin. I'm sure that's what you want to know."

She shook he head. "No, I'd like to know if he is."

"It's okay, Emme," Francis said. "Your folks grilled me about my lifestyle the whole time you were asleep. I might as well answer that one, too."

He turned to Mama. "I'm not a virgin, Mrs. Washington, but that doesn't mean Jean-Paul was altogether accurate. I know a lot of musicians full of integrity. He does have a point about some of us artists, however, and I bought into that same raggedy lifestyle when I was younger. All it brought was heartache and emptiness. I've changed. Inasmuch as I can, I walk with God. I'm not a perfect man, but I've been a gentleman when it comes to Emme."

"Tell us more about how you're not perfect," Jean-Paul said.

"Can you just stop riding a brotha?" I said. "What is any of this to you?"

"*Ma chère!* I'm merely doing what your big brother would if you brought a homeless, uneducated, jobless musician home and implied he could take care of you in any way other than . . . well, I think you know."

I was outraged! "May I remind you again that I'm an only child. I don't have a brother, nor do I need a surrogate one. Francis freelances making beats. He's about to sign a huge record deal, and he's only homeless because his father just died."

"Ah, *pardonnes moi*! I did not mean to imply your 'freelancing,' homeless, uneducated ghetto cliché hip-hop artist 'producer,' who lived off his father until his unfortunate death, is incapable of providing for and protecting you."

"Francis didn't live off his father. He helped *him*. His father was a priest!"

"A priest? A *Catholic* priest? With a son? Say it isn't so!"

I bit my lip. I had totally put Francis's business out there, but Francis already looked defeated.

"You did better than I did," he said. "After the three of them, I don't even like me for you."

"What happened out here?"

Jack looked at me, his eyes reassuring. "We just got to know one another."

"They don't know you at all, Francis."

Mama chimed in. "I'm sure Francis is a nice young man, and I appreciate all that he's done for you, but honey, you have a home now. You don't have to rush into getting married."

You'd think I'd have pounced on her again, since she's the one who rushed into getting married. But her words wrapped their arms around me and cooed assurances I didn't realize I needed.

I don't have to rush into getting married.

Being a man of impeccable timing, Jean-Paul pounced on my lack of reaction.

"Welcome home, Emme!"

I refused to look at that trash-talking creep. But I couldn't look at Francis either. It was enough to feel his disappointment burning into me. To his credit neither a whimper nor a roar came out of his mouth. Several awkward minutes passed before he finally stood and excused himself.

"I'm grateful to have met you all," he said, "but I'm going to be going now. Despite your low opinion of me and my future, I know God is with me, and I'm going to have a fantastic life. *With* Emme.

"I'm going to take a walk and then go over to see my friends at Sweet Lorraine's Jazz Club. And you can be assured that tonight I'll be settin' the joint on fire with my highly regarded music. They don't require me to book in advance. That's how good I am. You can say what you want, or believe what you will, but I know who I am, what I'm capable of, and how I'm going to do it."

He finished with, "Emme, if I may speak to you before I go?"

"Let me get my diva boots."

I'd taken them off in the guest bedroom and went to retrieve them. Francis followed me into the room and closed the door behind us.

"Better not do that. Jean-Paul will swear we're in here gettin' busy."

"Jean-Paul is about to catch a beat down."

I sat on the bed and pulled on one of my boots.

"You know I love you," Francis said.

"Fo' shizzle. I love you, too."

He placed his hand on my shoulder as if the gesture would anchor me to my mama's house. "You don't have to put on your diva boots. I'll bring your things over later."

"I'm going with you."

"No, you're not."

My face searched his. "What's the matter, baby?"

"That isn't what you want."

"That's crazy! Of course I want to be with you."

"I know you love me, Emme, but . . ." He seemed to wrestle with himself. I sat there scarcely breathing, my heart racing.

"But what, Francesco?"

"Never mind." He was quiet for a minute, as if he were shoring himself up to do something very difficult. "Listen, your folks ain't feeling me, and you need some time with your mother. Jack, too."

"You aren't worried about them out there, are you? Like, *really?*"

"I need to think, Emme. I'm just going to make some music."

"I want to go with you." I tried to slip on my other boot but he stopped my hand.

"I'll see you soon. Remember how we roll: watch and pray, Exorsistah."

"Please don't go."

"I wish you could be honest with yourself." He kissed me on my forehead and walked out of the room.

I sat there dumbfounded. Believe it or not, just like that I let the man I loved, the one who'd given me everything I'd ever wanted, leave without me.

Chapter Twelve

Before I had time to process what had just gone on, Jean-Paul appeared at the guest-room door with that goofy, annoying grin on his face.

"Don't look so brokenhearted, *ma soeur*; he'll be back."

I slid my other boot on. A sistah needed her diva boots around a man like that. "What's it to you?"

"I'm an Emmephile. What can I say? Mama Abby has told me stories about you since she arrived in our fair city. I never thought you'd show up here with a *beau*, but I should have. He was much too comfortable, *ma chère*. I gave him some incentive to stay on his toes, *oui*?"

"What makes you think we needed your help?"

Jean-Paul laughed. "He walked out of here without you. And you? You did not stop him. Perhaps you need more help than you think."

Mama peeked her head into the room before I could tell him off. "Are you hungry, baby?"

Jean-Paul answered yes at the exact time I said no.

What? I thought. *Is he her baby, too?*

Jack came up behind her. "I see you two are going to get along just fine. Jean-Paul, go out with me to get some provisions. We gon' have us our *réveillon* tonight."

"Could somebody please tell me what a *réveillon* is? That's the second offer I've had for one since I've been here."

"It's an old New Orleans tradition where we have a big dinner on Christmas Eve after Mass, but we'll get an early start for you, Em."

"Nobody calls me Em but my mama," I said to Jack. Again.

He smiled, not unlike his grinning fake son. "Maybe it's time for that to change."

With Jean-Paul and Jack out of the way, Mama and I were left with the awkwardness of being virtual strangers. Several times we attempted conversation before one of us hit a sensitive spot in the other. Fortunately, without our referees on hand, neither of us probed the other too deeply. We spent waaaay too much of our time silent. In one of those uncomfortable lulls my attention went back to the pictures on the wall. I thought of Celestine, coming to me so often, and wondered what was beleaguering my mama.

"What were your dreams like?" I asked. "The ones that brought you here."

She sank into the sofa, her shoulders rounded. "Terrifying."

"Do you ever dream about Celestine?"

"Not at all. Why would you ask me that?"

"I just wondered."

"It's not her in my nightmares."

More silence stretched between us, until I worked up the courage to ask another hard question.

"Do you still see them?" I didn't have to say what to her.

"No. Do you?"

"Yeah, I do. You mentioned you had skills. What are they if you don't see them anymore?"

"You can say the word 'demons' around me,

Emme." She sighed. "I have dreams that tell me things, but not everything. In many ways I'm as much in the dark with them as I would be without them."

"What good is a gift like that if you can't get the full picture?"

"I don't think I want to know the full picture."

She ain't never lied about that. I leaned closer to her. I had so many questions. It was hard to figure out where to begin.

"Did Ms. Jane ever tell you why you were targeted for demonic attack?"

Mama picked up her wineglass and took a sip. "She didn't have to tell me that."

"Why didn't you say anything to me?"

"You were frightened enough. So was I."

"How could you stand to look at me? Knowing? Remembering? Do I look like him?"

"I don't remember." She sat up straighter. "You see these television shows where women say they'll never forget the face of the man who raped them. But I could. I didn't want to remember him."

For the first time since we'd hugged at the door, Mama touched me. She reached over and stroked my hair.

"It was foolish of me to try to make a deal with the devil. I was young, alone, and traumatized, and those terrible things kept trying to hurt my baby. And you were *my* baby. Not the product of a rape, but a spectacular beauty from ashes gift. I wanted to protect you. All we had was each other."

"I thought that was how it would always be, Mama."

"So did I. But we were wrong, and that's good! It's a good thing to let other people love us. There really is strength in numbers."

I thought about my girls back home, Ndidi, Ty, and Kosha, and how they had had my back in the biggest battle of my life. "Yeah. It is."

Mama took another sip of Merlot and seemed to lose herself in memories.

"I forget sometimes how young you were when I got sick. You don't know many facts about me. I always thought I'd have a chance to tell you when you were older."

"I'm older."

She smiled. "So you are."

"I don't remember much family being around us," I said. "I had a couple of cousins, and there was that lady . . ."

"Those weren't your real cousins, Emme. They were my foster parents' grandchildren."

"You were in foster care? How come I never knew that?"

"I never wanted you to know, but I was lucky. Some decent people took care of me. To me, they were family."

"Why were you in the system?"

"I was alone. I don't know much about either side of my family. My parents were teens when my mother got pregnant. Nothing came of their relationship. Her parents disowned her because of me, and she didn't talk about them. Mama died in a car accident when I was in high school. That's how I got into the system. Fortunately, it worked for me. But I went on my way as soon as I was grown."

"I know what that's like. I stopped hiding on my birthday."

"Why did you run away, baby. Was it that bad?"

Bad was not the word for it. "Right now it's your turn."

A wistful expression softened her pretty features. "I was a student at Eastern Michigan University. I paid my own way, of course, had a scholarship, and worked at a pizza parlor on Washtenaw. At the time I lived on campus in an old Victorian house that had been converted into apartments." She sighed. "I loved Ypsi; I felt safe there. But one night, coming from studying at the library, I felt this ominous sense of dread. It was winter, so it got dark early, and I tried to rush home, to get off the streets."

I wondered if that dread she felt indicated some gift of knowledge lurking in her spirit. "Had you ever experienced precognitive intuitions before?"

"I wouldn't make this something it isn't, Emme."

"All right. Scratch that. Go on with your story."

Now anxiety pinched her features. "He grabbed me as I was coming through the hall that led to my apartment. I'd never known such evil as I saw in his face."

"But you don't remember what he looked like?"

"That's a mercy, Emme. Or at least it was."

"What do you mean?"

"Let's leave it at that for now."

Mama crossed her arms around her chest, as if her heart needed protection. "I don't remember much about what happened to me after the rape. He choked me until I lost consciousness. I know he took me somewhere, and there was this odd room that had the most bizarre symbols on the walls, and even the floor and ceiling. He had some of them on his body, and they were not like tattoos. The marks were raised like welts."

Okay, now she was seriously creeping me out. I didn't think it was a good time to show her the distinctive patterns on my chest. But Saint Michael had assured me they came from God. Archangels didn't lie.

I managed to mumble, "For real? Marks, huh?" unsure if I should prod her about his tripped-out body art, or if it even mattered. What insight would it give me?

"I don't even know how I got back home," she said. "The possession diminished me in many ways. I'm not like Jane. Once she was free, all of her memories were intact. It didn't happen that way for me."

"Jane said he offended his god, a demon the Bible calls—"

"The wicked demon Asmodeus. I know all about him, and the knowledge didn't come from Jane."

I wanted to tell her I knew all about him, too. And that Jane said he lusted for me, and his minions dogged me, bringing a whole lot of trouble with men, but the truth is, I'd hurt her enough with the junk that came out of my mouth. I also wondered if Jane Doe told Mama her little girl had been molested by four different men. Would that news have broken her heart, like the news that I was a rape baby broke mine? Then again, Jane was a wily one. She told only what she thought you needed to know.

"Mama," I said, moving closer to her on the sofa. "I know all of this is hard for you. It is for me, too, like, crazy hard. But I really need to know, was the man who raped you, the dude who fathered me, the person you were dreaming of? Is he the reason why you're here?"

The room went cold as a tomb; an exaggerated ripping noise startled me into hyperalert. I whipped my head around in time to see every photograph of Celestine Nuit being torn to shreds by hideous black claws that looked like they were made of smoke.

Mama gasped. "Oh, God help me! I can't go through it again. It'll kill me if it happens again." The terror in her face pissed me off.

"Mama," I said, cradling her face in my hands. "You're going to be all right. You've got this. Okay? There isn't a devil in hell that's going possess, oppress, or distress you ever again. So help *me* God."

I got up from that sofa and got ready to rumble.

Chapter Thirteen

The first thing a sistah had to do, especially since I'd spent the last few hours cutting a fool on grown folks, was repent.

"Lord, I'm sorry for the way I talked to my . . . parents. And even Jean-Paul, though you know he deserved it. I ask that you wash me in your blood. I'm heartily sorry for my sins, and I'm gonna get back to you in confession. But for now, cover me, Jesus. 'Cause I'm about to do my job."

The Scriptures tell us in II Corinthians 10:3–4,

"Indeed we live as human beings, but we do not wage war according to human standards; for the weapons of our warfare are not merely human, but they have divine power to destroy strongholds."

It was time to pull out my arsenal, starting with the whole armor of God.

"I, Emme Kate Vaughn, put on God's armor to resist the devil's tactics. I stand my ground with truth buckled around my waist and integrity for a breastplate. Faith is my shield, to put out the burning arrows of the evil one. I accept the salvation you freely give as my helmet and take the word of God revealed by the Holy Spirit as my sword."

Ready, I trooped over to Celestine's ruined photographs like the solider in the army of the Lord I was, firing the Anima Christi from my lips.

"Soul of Christ, sanctify me; body of Christ, save me; blood of Christ, inebriate me; water from the side of Christ, wash me; passion of Christ, strengthen me; o good Jesus, hear me; within your wounds, hide me; let me never be separated from you; from the evil one, protect me; at the hour of my death, call me; and bid me to come to you; that with your saints, I may praise you forever and ever. Amen."

It didn't hurt to ask for a little help from your friends: "Saint Michael the Archangel, defend us in battle. Be our protection against the wickedness and snares of the devil. May God rebuke him, we humbly pray, and do thou, o prince of heavenly hosts, by the divine power of God, cast into hell Satan, and all the evil spirits who roam throughout the world, seeking the ruin of souls. Amen."

I'd made it mad now, and the smoke morphed into smoky black dots and spread over the wall. That was a new one, and I thought I'd seen it all.

That's where I made my mistake. I was standing there looking at all these dots, wondering if that junk was gonna leave a stain, when those circles became cylinders and shot out at a sister like arrows, flattening me. They felt like needles piercing me.

"Aw, heck-e-naw!" I was gonna have to call on everybody.

"In the name of the Lord Jesus Christ, strengthened by the intercession of his mother the Virgin Mary, of blessed Michael the Archangel, of the blessed apostles Peter and Paul, and of all the saints and angels of heaven, powerful in the holy authority of the name of the Lord Jesus Christ, and by my authority as the Exorsistah, I ask my heavenly Father to rebuke this spirit of whatever the heck kind of evil this is, and to command it in the name of the Lord Jesus Christ to depart from this household, now, quietly, without harm to anyone."

It went quietly all right, but not without drama. What was left of Celestine's pictures flared into an enormous orange flame, which disappeared as quickly as it came, taking everything else off that part of the wall, including the paint.

The front door flew open, and a puff of black smoke whooshed out.

"Showoff."

Still. Devils don't go easy. I was going to have to fortify myself, my mama, and her and Jack's home. And I needed some wisdom because a couple of questions nagged at me. Why of all things did that devil choose the pictures to attack? And why did it happen as soon as I prodded her about the dream she'd been so reluctant to talk about?

I turned to Mama. "You all right?"

She nodded. "How did you do that?"

"I had to go to demon school. I picked up a few things."

Jack and Jean-Paul wandered through the open door.

"What was that coming out of my house?" Jack said. He abruptly dropped his bag of groceries onto the floor and went to Mama.

"That was things getting interesting around here," I answered. Jean-Paul set his groceries down on the coffee table and came to me. He cradled my elbow.

"Are you okay, *chérie*?"

"I'm good. I'm mad! But I'll be a'ight, and for future reference keep your hands off me."

He backed away, looking decidedly more engaged than offended.

Jack had knelt in front of Mama. "Abby, what happened?"

"I don't know. We were talking and suddenly the pictures started to . . ." She shook her head as if the gesture would knock the memory of it out of her mind.

"Have any other strange phenomena been happening in this house?" I asked.

"Like what?" Jack replied.

"Anything: cabinets opening by themselves, or the temperature inexplicably dropping; have you smelled any foulness that doesn't seem to have a source or heard weird noises, especially in the middle of the night?"

"No." He thought for a moment. "The only thing that's troubling to us is Abby's nightmares."

I put my hands on my hips. "Okay, what is up with the nightmares? As soon as I asked her about the dreams that brought her here a devil turned Celestine's pictures into Shredded Wheat."

My new stepfather's shoulders rounded and he

sighed like Francis does when everything gets to be a bit much for him to handle. "The dreams that brought her here were about . . ." He paused, like, forever.

"About what? What does a sistah have to do to get a straight answer around here?"

Jean-Paul was happy to oblige me. "They were about the man who fathered you, *chérie*. Now that you are here, perhaps the stakes have been raised."

"Mama, is that true?"

"I don't want to deal with this right now." She jumped up from the couch and stormed out of the room, Jack trailing behind her.

Jean-Paul's mouth eased into a sly grin. Dude was so stinkin' beautiful. His smile affected me the way Francis's golden eyes do, and despite my anger I found my guard slipping, just a little, but it was enough to give him an in. And he knew it.

"*Venez avec moi?*" he said.

My hands remained on my hips. "What does that mean?"

"It means come with me. I think some air would be good for you."

I had no idea why I was doing it, but I followed him outside. The rain had returned, shrouding the air. We stood out in the drizzle, but it felt as good as it had when I woke up that morning and had my impromptu worship session. For a while neither of us spoke. Finally Jean-Paul's sarcasm cut through our silence.

"Emme?"

I wondered what would come out if his mouth now. "What?"

"I don't want to embarrass you, but there is something you need to know. I'm afraid it is of a personal nature."

I eyed him warily. "What are you talking about, Jean-Paul."

"You have spots all over your face."

"Oh no!" I grazed my hands across my face. I could actually feel them! "Awwwww *man*! I *hate* demons!"

Jean-Paul just laughed, like he thought the whole thing was a joke.

Chapter Fourteen

It's an understatement to say that I found yet another kind of supernatural signature left on my body distressing. I ran back into the house, with Jean-Paul on my heels. The bathroom mirror confirmed that I looked like a dark-skinned Dalmatian, and Jean-Paul stood behind me enjoying the whole fiasco. He could hardly contain his mirth.

"May I touch them, Emme? I find them fascinating."

"You keep your hands away from me, Jean-Paul! Always trying to touch somebody."

"But I like you. You're . . . diverting. *Je vous trouve drôle.*"

"Stop talking Creole."

"*Ce qui était français, ma chère.*"

I glared at him.

"I said, 'That was French, my dear.'"

"How do you say 'you annoy me' in French?"

He made a sweeping gesture with his hand. "Eh, you can say, *'Je veux apprendre à mieux vous connaître, Jean-Paul. Vous me l'intrigue.'*"

I turned away from my spotty image in the mirror. "Call me crazy, Jean-Paul, but that whole *l'intrigue* thing doesn't sound like you told me how to say 'you annoy me' in French."

He flung his hands up, conceding—at least I thought so.

As obnoxious as he was, his charms blunted my sharp edge.

"*Viens ici.*" He reached for me. "Let me see if they come off. Come."

I felt something stirring in my belly, an odd attraction and repulsion in equal measure. He moved closer and took my face in his hands. Gently—no, exquisitely—he caressed each spot with the pads of his thumbs. Heat spread out from his hands into my face. Or was that me blushing?

"Please . . . Don't, Jean-Paul."

He splayed his long fingers and traced a path down my face: from my forehead to my neck and onto my shoulders, where his hands finally rested. "There," he said. With a nudge, he urged me to turn back to the mirror. Every one of the spots was gone, leaving my skin with a luminous cast.

I faced him again, mesmerized by this demonstration. "Who are you?"

The intensity in his eyes scared me.

"Je suis ton autre."

I didn't ask him what he said. His words sounded too urgent. I tried to blot the foreign words from memory, like my mama erased the face of the man who raped her.

Chapter Fifteen

Jean-Paul asked me to walk with him. How was I supposed to refuse him after he'd healed me? I didn't want to show my apprehension about being alone with him, so I put on my tough sistah act and feigned apathy.

"Whatever. Let me get my jacket."

I fortified myself against the elements; he didn't bother, and we stepped out into the gray. I knew St. Anna's was nearby, but I didn't want to see the murder board again. Fo' sho' I didn't want Celestine to pop up, since she never seemed to do anything but bring me trouble.

"Don't worry, Emme."

Now he was really creeping me out. "Don't worry about what?" I said evenly.

"About anything, *chère*."

"Where's the nearest Catholic church?"

Again he chuckled like I'd said something amusing. "A few blocks from here. I'll take you."

He stuck his elbow out for me to hook my arm onto, but I wasn't feeling that.

"Emme, you wouldn't deny me the opportunity to be a southern gentleman, would you?"

"No offense, Jean-Paul, but I'm really not the touchy-feely type."

"What's wrong with touching? Did you not find it beneficial when I touched you in the bathroom?"

"Yes, I did. But I don't have any spots on my face now."

"I can put them back." He flashed his stunning smile again.

"I'm gonna pass on that."

He didn't budge. "Human beings crave contact. Studies have been done with those little baby monkeys; the ones whose mothers didn't touch them didn't do so well. Some of them died."

"I'm not a primate."

"Technically you are, and you, too, long to be touched. You must be so weary of your defenses keeping you from intimacy. I don't want anything but to help you get to church so God can touch you, but surely I've proven God also does that through the people who care about you."

"You don't care about me," I said, even though everything he said was spot on. No pun intended.

Again, he flashed that maddening smile. "*Au contraire.* I've been waiting for you for a long time."

I took a deep breath. "Look, Jean-Paul. You're strange, and I have no idea what you did to me back there, but if you're trying to get with me, I have nothing for you. I love Francis. We're engaged to be married and faithful to each other."

"You're upset, Emme. Let's go talk to the good Lord. You will like the church I'm going to take you to, *ma soeur.*"

"You didn't just call me a cabbage, did you?"

He chuckled. "*Non.*"

"What does *'ma soeur'* mean?"

"My sister."

"You aren't my brother."

He shrugged his broad shoulders. "I've always wanted a sister. I grew up in an orphanage. You can't blame me for trying."

It troubles me now how easily I slid my arm

through his. I told myself all he was doing was showing me where a church was. I stuffed the thought that anything else was happening into some dark corner of my psyche and hoped it would stay there, being very, very quiet.

Chapter Sixteen

According to Jean-Paul it would only take a few minutes to reach St. Augustine's. He filled the time with a history lesson.

"St. Augustine's is the oldest black Catholic church in the country. It was actually built on Claude Tremé's plantation. Free black slaves established it, but they bought pews for slaves so they could attend, too."

"What do you mean they bought pews?"

"Ah, *chérie*. A long time ago, if you wanted to go to church, you had to purchase your seat! So, before the dedication of the church—this was in the mid 1800s—free blacks bought pews for their families. But whites decided they would buy more pews so they wouldn't have to worship with a lot of blacks. This started the great War of the Pews."

His voice was fluid. So was the way he talked with his hands. "The free blacks bought three pews for every one that white people bought. They ended up with all the pews on the side aisles. This was a big deal, *chérie*, because they gave those pews to slaves and established the most integrated congregation in America. There was a long pew full of free blacks, and a long pew of whites. On the two outer aisles the slaves worshipped."

I couldn't help but smile at the astute moves the free blacks made. Talk about black power! "That rocks, Jean-Paul."

"That rocks hard, *demi-soeur*."

The building was white, with an impressive, though damaged belltower.

"Katrina?" I asked.

Jean-Paul slung his arm around my shoulder, which almost made me hyperventilate, but I stayed calm. "*Oui*, the roof, too. If we don't raise enough money to repair it, the church may be forced to close down. The archdiocese has been gunning for us to close for years."

"Is this the church you attend?"

"Oh yes. I wouldn't think to go anywhere else in this city. There's too much history here. I'm a real history buff, *mademoiselle*. Knowing your roots is powerful. That's one reason our doors are still open. We know who we are here." His gaze flickered over me. "Do you know who you are?"

"What? Am I acting like I have amnesia?"

"The question goes deeper than knowing the basic facts about yourself. It's a question like a river, *cher*—deep and wide. Do you know who you *are*?"

I slipped away from him and stepped back, as if I were taking in a broader view. "This building is hype. Are we going inside or what?"

"We're going inside. Unless you'd prefer the *what*."

When I didn't say a word he made a sweeping gesture toward the front entrance. "This way." I didn't take his arm.

The front entrance was lovely. "Wow."

"You like?"

"Yeah. I mean, it's no St. Louis Cathedral, but it's so beautiful."

He laughed. "It was designed by J. N. B. de Pouilly. The same architect."

"I knew I dug it for a reason."

That de Pouilly was one bad dude. I was struck by this building's simplicity, compared to the opulent cathedral in the French Quarter. A line of rectangular stained-glass windows stretched across the white brick like dashes. The sides of the building were dotted with intermittent circles of stained glass, their colors richer and brighter than the front entrance's windows. The door was light-colored carved wood, maybe oak, which swung open to a welcoming nave.

It was the sanctuary that made me gasp. It had de Pouilly's reaching-for-God columns with their gilded tops, only St. Augustine's had no galleries. Nor did it have a domed ceiling of icons. What it did boast of, however, alternating between the stained glass and stations of the cross, were the coolest collection of photographs and original art right there on the walls. I'll bet that French architect wouldn't have thought of doing that! The pictures depicted black life with the clarity of Stevie Wonder's *Songs in the Key of Life* album. A totally funky painting of Louis Armstrong blowing his trumpet hung next to photographs of regular folks in a whole spectrum of colors in the African-American rainbow. Some wore traditional African finery. Others were dressed in plain clothes like your everyday plaid shirt. These photographs were icons, too.

Sunlight streamed through the round stained-glass windows, while lamps illuminated the outer aisles. One of the altars, a piece of art if there ever was one, was made of tree trunks. I felt more at home in that sanctuary than I had anywhere for a while, and I wished Francesco were with me to share it, instead of Jean-Paul.

When we sat down on one of the outer pews, I thought of those slaves and the freedom I had to worship wherever I want to. "Thank you, Lord."

Jean Paul sat beside me, giving thanks himself. He made the sign of the cross and it oddly comforted me. I felt a little self-conscious with him beside me. Prayer was kinda intimate, and the dude already had me thinking about how much I needed to be touched. But too much was at stake for me to be trippin'. My mama was at risk, and where two or three were gathered in the Lord's name, he was there in the midst. I had to woman up.

"Would you mind praying with me, Jean-Paul?"

He took my hand in his, and I bowed my head and closed my eyes. For the second time in my life, I felt a jolt of something like electricity surge through me, binding me to another person. I yanked my hand away, but it was too late.

Oh man. God opened Jean-Paul's heart and allowed me inside it, that poor baby. Sorrow had kept its heavy hand on his head since he was a knee-high guy. Behind that fetching façade was a person with a lot of pain.

When I looked up I found him staring at me.

"*Ma soeur?*" he said calmly.

I didn't answer.

"This is most disturbing, *oui*?"

"I've seen worse."

But he wanted to talk about me. "Grotesque, abominable creatures chased you. I saw them as clearly as I'm seeing you now. I am a man of many experiences, but that has never happened to me. Remarkable."

"It's me who chases the demons now. I send them right back to whatever hell they came from."

"You are a treasure trove of powerful gifts. That could be useful, *oui*?"

"Whatever. I felt your sadness, Jean-Paul, when you were a little boy."

"I grieved for my mother."

"You were there when she was murdered, weren't you?"

"Obviously I was." His mouth twitched, the first sign I'd seen of a crack in his veneer. "What do we do with this?"

"I don't know." I said.

God, what are you doing? I wanted to ask, but I

wouldn't pray that out loud. The words in my prayer book came to mind. With thanksgiving, and no touching, I began to pray what was comfortable and familiar:

"O God, come to my assistance. O Lord, make haste to help me."

The words loosened my tongue. Petitions poured out of me. I gave Jesus just about everything I had, begging him for protection for my mama; for strength; for allies, because I knew we couldn't do anything alone. I petitioned him to show me *exactly* what I was supposed to do. After that, the only thing left to do was drink in the quiet and store it inside me like a cactus does water.

Jean-Paul didn't say a word as I prayed. I should have noted that, but all I did was tell myself some people aren't very vocal when they pray, and try to believe it.

Chapter Seventeen

After prayer I wanted to get back to the house, but Jean-Paul insisted on showing me one more thing. He took my hand again and almost dragged me toward the back of St. Augustine's.

"Wait! Where are you tryna to take me?" The feeling that I was in a scary movie was back, and I was the dumb girl some guy was trying to do something freaky to before they both got killed.

"Stop being ridiculous. I want to show you something."

I dug my heels in. *"What?"*

He didn't grin at me that time. I'd finally managed to irk him. "It's a shrine, and you may rest assured I have no intention of sexually assaulting you. I am *not* the men who molested you."

My stomach felt like it dropped to the toes of my diva boots, and this time I was completely unable to dredge up any false bravado. He did that junk on purpose. Interesting. I knew his soft spot, and he knew mine. We circled each other like a couple of predators prepared to attack. I balled my fists for the sole reason that it made me feel better.

Finally he ran his hand across his precision haircut. "It's only a shrine. Will you please come with me and take a look at it?"

"Don't tell Mama about the men who hurt me."

"Don't bring up what you did to me again. Ever."

"Fine with me." I followed him to the back of the building.

Nestled in a browned and sleeping garden, a cross rose out of the rock-strewn ground. It was made of the biggest, thickest rusted chain I'd ever seen, positioned as if Jesus had carried it on his shoulder then abruptly fell to his knees, overburdened by its weight. One crossbar touched the ground; the other rose toward the sky. Open shackles and a ball and chain dangled from it, as if folks who had been bound to it were suddenly freed, leaving their fetters behind. Smaller rusted metal crosses, like the kind you'd see at a memorial site, surrounded it.

A wave of nausea hit me.

"Are you ill, Emme?"

"No." But I felt like I was spinning on the inside. My heart seemed to throb in my throat.

"What is all this?" I said. A noose hung on one of the tree limbs, and a shudder went through me, shaking me to the core. My knees buckled and I fell to the ground. A chorus of voices seemed to come from my belly.

I know art can be powerful, but not enough to make you hear whispers. Hundreds of them chattered within me. They weren't demon voices. These demanding, insistent spirits felt human, which made them even scarier to me.

Oh, Jesus. I touched that stupid ghost, and now all kind of spirits have possessed me. I ain't tryna be no channel. What's happening to me?

Some voices were angry, others resigned, and everything in between babbled inside me. When it felt like they'd burst out of me like Ripley's inner invader in the *Alien* movies, I held my midsection and heaved from my empty stomach until bile spilled out of my mouth.

"Oh, God, help me!"

Jean-Paul knelt beside me, stroking my hair. "There, there, *ma pauvre chérie*. This is the tomb of the unknown slave. The voices you're hearing are the ancestors. They want to be heard. They are demanding justice. Listen to me carefully, Emme. You are going to be very uncomfortable for the next few days. At times you are going to think you are going insane, but it is not so. The gifts inside you that you have forgotten are being awakened. Do not be afraid."

I heard him as if he were speaking through water. A vortex whirled around my insides. I slumped into Jean-Paul's arms. A blessed nothingness washed over me and everything faded to bright white.

Chapter Eighteen

I woke up in a strange bed with blinding white linens and a mattress so incredibly comfortable that it made me want to curl up and go back to sleep. So the bed wasn't strange. I just had no idea who it belonged to, or why I was in it.

My head still hurt, and I widened my eyes and blinked to sharpen my focus. I tried to fish memories of the last few hours from my murky consciousness.

"Jean-Paul!" I bolted up with a start and felt like my head would split in two.

"There's no need to yell," a woman's voice said. "I'm blind, not deaf."

The freakin' Oracle, wearing Blues Brothers sunglasses and sipping a cup of tea, sat in a rocking chair beside me.

"Aw, shoot! Now I'm hallucinating that I'm in the Matrix!"

She chuckled. "I get that all the time. No, *chérie*. You're not in the Matrix. I just look a whole lot like Gloria Foster. I've got the same wide body and pretty face, and my hair is wavy and bobbed like she used to wear hers. I like wearing a bob. I don't have to do much to it, and my husband says I still look good. That's important if you're blind. I haven't always been blind, you know.

"Oh, and I don't smoke cigarettes, and I don't bake cookies. Predicting the future isn't my strong suit either, but I have been known to see a few things other folks can't see, and sometimes the Lord gives me inside information. That makes people think I can tell them the future, but the truth is, I'm just plain old Mary Brooks on St. Claude Avenue who the good Lord talks to sometimes. I live three doors down from the church. Jean-Paul brought you here. He thought I'd be able to help you."

Why does her name sound familiar?

Jean-Paul leaned against the doorjamb, watching us.

"I'm okay, Ms. Mary," I said. "I just have a really bad headache. I don't need you to help me with anything."

She snickered and called out to Jean-Paul. "She's acting just like you said she would, J-P."

I gave him my iciest stare. "What did *J-P* tell you, Ms. Mary?"

"He told me about your gift."

"What gift?"

Jean-Paul spoke. "You mean *which* gift, *ma soeur*; you have many."

Before I could respond to the bane of my existence, the Oracle sighed like she was tired of me already. "I'm going to help you with the visions you're having of the dead."

Okay. I don't tell anybody about my ability to see the dead. Francis knew, but that was about it. And exactly how much of me could Jean-Paul see? I kicked the covers off and tried to jump out of bed, but dizziness took hold of me and I fell back onto the pillows.

Jean-Paul was at my side as fast as Jack made it to my mother when he found us looking crazy and staring at the wall. "Stay on the bed, girl. You're not ready yet."

"Ready for what? I want to go! I need to see Francis."

"I'll take you to him when you're stronger. I promise. Right now you need to listen."

Because I was too weak to have any choice in the matter, I rested my back against a pillow that cushioned me from the ornate headboard. Jean-Paul sat beside me. I was all too aware of him and the weird connection we shared.

"Okay, since I'm a captive audience, what?" I didn't bother to hide my hostility.

Ms. Mary started. "The first thing I want you to know is that you're among friends. You can drop the girl-against-the-world bit. The second thing is, I want you to know that everyone is unique. There isn't a single duplicate in the whole lot of us. C. S. Lewis said our souls are made to fit particular swellings in the infinite contours of divine substance. You, child, are designed to know for all eternity some aspect of divine beauty better than any other creature can." She paused and took another sip of tea. "That was what Lewis said. Now Ms. Mary is gonna talk to you."

She turned her face toward the bed as if she could see me. "Your *beau* here tells me you've been seeing spirits since you were a little girl."

"He's not my *beau*. And what I saw were demons."

"Are you sure it was only demons, *chérie*?"

Mary's face was soft and motherly. In some way, she reminded me of my mama, or maybe what I imagined my grandmother would have been like. She had a face that compelled me to be honest.

"I don't talk about this with anyone."

"I understand that. Neither did I, until I felt like I would go cuckoo if I didn't understand this thing. You're lucky. I didn't have a Mary Brooks in my life to talk about these matters with. I had to muddle along on my own, picking up bad advice from insipid occult books until I was almost forty years old. Now tell me what you saw when you were a girl. Not the demons. The other folks, when it first started."

I closed my eyes. It had been a really long time since I allowed myself to think of such a thing. In my imagination I tried to place myself—anxiety, uncertainty, and all—into the quiet I'd tucked inside myself when I prayed at St. Augustine's.

I made the sign of the cross. "God, protect me," I prayed. "I don't know what I'm doing here."

When I felt the warmth of his presence, I tried to open up like a bud finally blooming. "Help me to remember, Jesus. What did I see?"

I'm six or seven years old. By now the demons harass me every night. Every time I tell Mama about it she feels more sad, so I don't want to tell her now. But the demons scare me. A lot.

I'm particularly afraid tonight. I say my prayers but stop midsentence and whisper in the dark, "I don't wanna be by myself." I put the covers over my head and curl up in a ball. And then the lady comes in and sits on my bed. We watch a church movie on my wall.

When I'm sleepy, she gets up to leave. She smiles and kisses me on my forehead. "Goodnight, Chiara," she says, and I fall asleep in perfect peace.

"Oh, man! I can't remember the last time I thought of that."

Mary's voice broke through my reverie. "So . . . you do remember something?"

"Yeah! A woman."

"What did she look like?"

I thought how Francis said ghosts tend to manifest. "Not like some kind of orb or anything. She seemed like a real lady, as real as you are."

"What was she wearing?"

"I thought she had on a funny nightgown back then, but now it seems like she had on . . . ." Mother Nicole came to mind. The first time I saw her I asked if she slept in her clothes. "She seemed to be wearing a nun's habit. And we watched church on the wall."

"What kind of church?"

"It was definitely a Mass. I remember all of this now, but when I was a kid, I had no idea what I was looking at."

"Did she speak?"

"She said, 'Goodnight, Chiara.'"

"Chiara? What does that mean?"

It all came clear as soon as she asked the question. I can't believe I didn't put all of this together before. "She called me Chiara because I'm her soul child. Chiara was her childhood name. Chiara Offreduccio. Later she would be called Saint Clare of Assisi."

Mary shook her head. "Umph, umph, umph. You were seeing the saints. Did she visit you often?"

"No, only when I was really, really afraid." I placed my hand over my heart. The most ardent gratitude began to fill me up. "Once she brought him with her. He didn't look like he does in the paintings. He was cute! And his hair was wild and curly, like he needed a haircut. He didn't wear the brown robe I see him in on holy cards, either. It was gray, and tattered. Both of them were barefoot. He made me laugh making animal sounds, and I almost got in trouble because Mama thought I was goofing around instead of going to sleep."

My revelations excited Jean-Paul. "Saint Francis of Assisi! Don't you see? Your gifts are more impressive than just seeing demons. You see saints!"

Mary interrupted. "And the dead. Tell me about that."

But I thought better of it. Jean-Paul knew about Celestine, and I didn't want to complicate things, especially for me! I focused on a few other dead folks I'd seen recently.

"When I was little, sometimes, these kinda sad, lost-looking wispy people would come into my room, but they never stayed long, and I never, you know, did anything for them. But recently, I saw a minister I know. He gave me a message that he wanted me to give to his son. After that I saw a friend of mine, a woman who means a lot to me. She didn't say anything, but her presence, just for a moment, was enough to let me know I had to do what I had to do. She was telling me, in her own way, to be fearless."

"Anybody else?" Mary said.

"He isn't dead, but . . . I saw the Lord. It was a vision of him, but it was so real. I know it was all of him I could stand, but it was him." I let out a breath. "Oh, Lord. What is this craziness? What happened to me at the church, Ms. Mary?"

"Here's the thing, sweetness. You're in New Orleans. It's what you call one of those thin places."

"Between heaven and hell. Why do people keep telling me that?"

"Maybe because we're closer to both than is comfortable for us mere mortals. What happened to you at the church was just overload. You didn't see any haints there, but it felt like you did because you were standing on holy ground. The bones of your ancestors lay in that soil. You tapped into their sorrow on a spiritual level. That'll clear up to a degree when you're used to being a sensitive, but you'll always feel much more than other folks."

"Oh, no! I'm not a sensitive. My fiancé is. I'm only like a sensitive when I'm close to him."

"Sweetness, you are a sensitive. You've always been. You just had your little hands full dealing with demons, so your other gifts stayed quiet. For whatever reason, they're being unlocked now. I told you I don't predict the future, but I can know what's happening right in front of me and can make some intelligent speculations, and I speculate that you're here to do some work that's going to require every bit of your abilities. It behooves you to get as much information as you can about what you're dealing with. If you aren't feeling like a grown-up, I suggest you throw that out of your head. As folk with common sense will tell you, it's time to put on your big-girl panties, because you've got some kind of job ahead of you, and it's the work of a strong woman, not a child."

"Thanks. This was fun, but I need to see my fiancé."

I tried to stand up, but Jean-Paul pushed me back on the bed. Not hard, but enough to irritate me.

"Sit."

"Quit playing, J-P!"

Ms. Mary shook her head at us. "You two are a mess, but I have to say, J-P is awfully fond of you. Have a cup of tea first, *chérie*. You'll need your strength." She turned to Jean-Paul. "Get this child some rosemary tea. It'll help her clear her head. She's gonna need all the clarity she can get."

She picked up her white cane, hefted herself out of the rocker, and tapped her way out of the room.

Chapter Nineteen

I had more clarity than I wanted. Seriously. Mary Brooks had given me a head full of insight that loosed memories I'd long suppressed. They continued to bubble up to consciousness, bringing alarming revelations. Emme Vaughn had a lot more dwelling within than anyone realized, and I needed to see Francesco, badly, just to help me make sense of things.

Something about Jean-Paul made me nervous, but I couldn't put my finger on what it was. At the same time, I felt oddly at home with him, like a little *too* comfortable. After we left Mary's I was ready to go to Francis, and Jean-Paul and I fought all the way to Sweet Lorraine's. Not that it was a long way. It was just down the street, but we argued passionately. Him because he thought I should have rested longer before he took me to the famous jazz club; me because I was sick of him.

Jean-Paul did have a point. I still felt wobbly, and the French Quarter was jumpin' at night. The press of crowds clamoring to get into the restaurants and clubs left me dizzy. My soul felt raw and opened wide, and the onslaught of empathy from the masses on the street had me hanging on tight to Jean-Paul's arm.

"Let me take you home, *chérie*," he said. Again.

"I need to see him."

"You shouldn't be absorbing all this energy. It's too much too soon. I'll talk to your *beau* after his gig and personally escort him back to the house. You can speak with him then."

"First: I don't want you alone with him. God only knows what you'll try to do. Second: it'll be too late then, and that'll just make things worse for everybody at the house. Mama knows I'm with you right now. Maybe she'll think we're making that indelible connection she was hoping for and she'll chill."

I didn't convince him, but he stopped fighting me. "As soon as you see him I'm taking you home. You don't understand what's happening to you, Emme."

"Oh, and you do?"

"More than you know."

Before I could pursue that insight further we were standing in front of what looked like an old row house that had been converted, added on to, and all kinds of other stuff over time. A neon sign in the window assured me we were at Sweet Lorraine's, and I didn't have to be inside to hear Francis *killing* the audience, doing things with a bass that you wouldn't believe were possible if you didn't hear it for yourself.

"That's him!" I said, excited. "He's playing the bass!"

Jean-Paul frowned. "He can't play like that."

"I'm telling you that's him! I'd know his sound anywhere."

He whistled. "He's wicked."

"Not my Francesco. He credits God with all of his talent, and every other gift he has." Something occurred to me. "Am I gonna have any trouble getting in here? I don't have any I.D. with me, and anyway, I'm only eighteen."

"You're with me, *chérie*. I come here all the time, and I don't bring babies with me."

"How old are you?"

"Old enough to show you things Francis hasn't, and young enough to make you like them."

My eyes widened. *"What?"*

A throaty laugh burst out of Jean-Paul. "I'm twenty-five. Does that make you feel better?"

"I'd feel more better if you didn't talk nasty to me."

"Your mind made it nasty. I never said what the things were."

"Can you just say very little to me in general?"

"I am most sorry, Emme. I do not want to offend you when we're just getting started."

"We aren't getting started with anything, okay? I'm not the one."

"Ah, but you are the one. You just don't know it. Now, are we going in to see your man, or what?"

"We're going in to see *my man*!"

True to his word, Jean-Paul ushered us into the club without a hitch. It seemed bigger on the inside than it did on the outside, and in my vulnerable state I didn't feel altogether comfortable in there. It was dark, and smoky, and full of grown folks.

"You're an adult, Emme," Jean-Paul said with a sigh.

"Cool it on the mind-reading thing. I'm not in love with it when Francis does it, but I hate it from you."

The night was young, and already the tables closest to the stage were filled. Jean-Paul wanted to try to find us a seat up front, but the fact that I was with him might not be something Francis wanted to see. I talked Jean-Paul into sitting in the back and wondered how I could get to Francis without him knowing Jean-Paul was with me.

"You have a real teeny-bopper soap opera going on, *ma soeur*. It is pathetic."

"Could you stop doing that, please?"

"I didn't read your mind. It is written all over your face, little girl."

I tried to glare at him and got an eyeful of delight. In the darkened club he possessed a transcendent beauty. He was definitely no little boy. At twenty-five he was not just crazy fine, but intelligent, worldly, and mad self-assured. In fact, he was way more confident than even Francis was, despite the sorrow I knew underlaid his allure.

I paused. I'd just compared him to Francis, and that disturbed me. There couldn't be any good end to that kind of thing. I turned my focus back to the music, a palpable thing, thrumming through my blood. The music would break the spell Jean-Paul seemed to be conjuring.

But he wasn't the only man in the room who was spellbinding. The two hundred or so people gathered in that joint were intoxicated, and not because they'd been drinking alcohol. I had never been to one of Francis's gigs. I'd seen him play at church, but never a nightclub. He always said I was too young to go with him, and apparently I was.

He was different on this kind of stage, a more sensual version of himself, exuding an animal energy he'd been very careful not to expose me to. I wasn't the only one who noticed. The women in the audience were flipping their weaves. One of them rushed the stage and put her arms around him, trying her best to get a kiss, until the security guard escorted her off.

"Did you see that?" I asked Jean-Paul, outraged.

He shrugged. "The ladies like him. Can you blame them? He's putting a hurting on that bass. I think *I'm* falling in love with him."

"She ran up on the stage and hung on him like an ornament on a Christmas tree."

"It's interesting that he didn't stop her."

"He was busy playing his music."

He shook his head and smirked.

"What?" I demanded.

"Keep telling yourself that, Emme. I'm sure that illusion will serve the little girl you think you are very well."

"I don't think I like what you're implying."

"Then maybe you need to get real. He's a jazz musician, like scores of others of that musical tribe around here. He's going to sign this record deal that you're so confident is going to secure your future, and he'll go on tour. Without you, *chérie*. You will be home having babies, sinking into depression, and letting your looks go, while nubile beauties, much more attractive than that woman is, offer themselves to him like he was a god. Between sets, they'll slip their phone numbers and panties in the pocket of his suit jacket, like that woman just did."

"She did not! And Francis would never be unfaithful to me."

"That's exactly what she did, and your Francis is a man, not a saint like his namesake. He's not immune to the lusts of the flesh. To tell you the truth, the way he rocks a house, wee one, he may have tasted forbidden fruit already, but you're too naïve to smell another woman on him."

His words silenced me. I watched the stage, refusing to look at Jean-Paul, while I wrestled with whether his glib predictions had any merit. Insecurity sank me into my chair. What did I have to offer Francis? How long would he be intrigued with me only because I had an unusual spiritual gift? Father Miguel was dead. Our exorcism team had been dismantled. What good was seeing demons now?

New Orleans was turning my whole world inside out. What in the heck-e-naw was going on? I was sitting in the club with another man while women were putting their panties in Francis's pocket, and I was doing absolutely nothing about it.

Chapter Twenty

By eleven o'clock I had my fill of Sweet Lorraine's. Too many other people's feelings, aches, and hungers had been foisted on my fragile psyche. When Jean-Paul and I stepped out into the night, the onslaught of their madness, and the fishy, rotten-smelling air hit me with such force I had cover my mouth, then run on rubbery legs behind a tree to puke my rosemary tea onto the grass.

"You aren't ready to be out," Jean-Paul said.

"Just take me to Baptiste Row Bed and Breakfast."

"For what?"

"That's where I'm staying tonight. With Francis."

"He's not there yet, and what about your mother? Don't you think she needs you more than he does? Your *beau* looks fine, but your mother is in bad shape. What about that prayer you had this morning while it rained?"

"Stop it! And how do you know I prayed outside in the rain?"

He chuckled. "I did not know. I guessed that you prayed because you are a person who prays, *oui*? And it rained all morning, so you had to pray while it was raining, if you prayed at all, though if I wanted to, I could have made you think I had answers you simply gave me. One day you will be able to read people based the reactions they have to the most basic inquiries. It is how many of your television evangelists operate. But there are true spiritual gifts that are not based on observation. Because I'm more seasoned in utilizing my gifts than you are, I have the advantage. That is why you cannot read Francis's thoughts like he can read yours, but we do not know all things. That is for God alone."

"So you know Francis is a sensitive?"

"*Oui*, and he knows I am one."

"He didn't tell me that."

"There is a lot he doesn't tell you, *chérie*."

"Like what?"

"He wants to marry you now. He is, how do I put this delicately? *Ready* for you." The degenerate's laugh even sounded lascivious.

"He loves me."

"I don't doubt that. He wishes to love you more."

"Shut up!"

"Too bad you are a child. But he is willing to wait for you, at least he is now. What will happen when he is on the road, one can only guess at. Would you like to hear my guess?"

"I'd like for you to take me to my mama."

"Of course you would."

Despite him being a butthead, Jean-Paul was at least right about my mama. I shouldn't have had to be convinced to be with the person I'd yearned for for three long years. But instead of thinking about her needs, I sulked every step of the way back to her house, wondering if Francis would have more panties than Victoria's Secret before the bartender shouted, "Last call."

Turns out Mama and Jack were early birds. Jean-Paul had a key to their place and let me in. He didn't stay, just planted a swift kiss on my cheek, winked at me, and waltzed out the door. By midnight I was in bed in the guest room, thankful to God that Mama was already asleep so I wouldn't have to deal with the pain of remembering her being bullied by a demon with a few punk parlor tricks.

"You are an awful person, Emme Vaughn," I said aloud. But God knows I was already feeling like I had when I was a kid: like I was the parent, and she was the child, and I had to be the one who made everything right. I wasn't ready to be the grown-up now.

"Lord, it's only so much I can stand. Slow my roll, 'cause I'm going round and round way too fast, and it's making me crazy."

That was one inadequate prayer.

I missed the comforting rhythms of the Psalms in my prayer book. I knew my mama had a Bible somewhere in that house, and every Bible I've ever seen with the Old Testament had the book of Psalms in it, so it wasn't really my prayer book I snuck out at three o'clock in the morning for.

I should have known better than to tip out at the witching hour in my condition. Running the streets at that time was always a bad idea, but the witching hour combined with the weird things happening to me was a recipe for a terrifying head-trip. Every sound was amplified. Creatures of the night, invisible to everyone else, rushed at me then retreated, laughing. I felt like I was in some demonic fun house, with nothing to hold on to. I was all so very strange, nothing like the usual stuff that plagued me at all.

"Mama?" I hadn't called on her in a long time. "I'm so sick. I need to lie down." I eased myself down onto the cold, wet brick road while hot tears slid past my temples. Evil hovered over me, preparing for attack, and I was helpless as a newborn baby.

"Jesus . . . Soul of Christ . . ." *What is the rest?*

Devils circled me like vultures.

"Saint Michael the Archangel, defend us in battle . . ." I couldn't remember the words. "Saint Michael . . . Brother?"

I felt so sleepy; I closed my eyes just for a moment to have a little rest.

I dreamed a man with strong arms picked me up. He crooned sweet talk in my ear.

"I was trying to get to Francesco," I said.

"I know, Chiara, I know," the voice said before I went to sleep.

Chapter Twenty-one

My eyes fluttered open, and predictably my head hurt. I wondered if I was allergic to thin places between heaven and hell. The ceiling was unfamiliar.

Lovely. Another unfamiliar bed, in another unfamiliar room. Where am I this time?

Francis's familiar scent filled me—vetiver and sandalwood. But it was mixed with an unpleasant metallic odor.

Anger?

Wait a minute. Since when have I been able to smell emotions?

I tried to sit up.

"Lie back down, X."

"Where are we, Francesco?"

His tone of voice was clipped. "We're in my room at *tante's*. I had to move out of the double, but this came available."

A pause, pregnant with his unexpressed fury, filled the space between us.

"Why are you so mad at me?" I asked.

"You were lying outside on the wet ground when I found you. This is the murder capitol, Emme. You saw the murder board yourself! Are you insane? And what were you doing out there, during the witching hour when you know all kinds of scavengers in the dark are prowling. Didn't he have the decency to see you home?"

"Who?"

"Don't play games with me, X. I don't deserve that."

"I was alone. I came from Mama's house."

"Yeah, right."

I made another brave attempt at sitting up.

"Lie down, X."

I had no choice really. "How did you find me?"

"Don't you know? It ain't only MapQuest that leads me to you."

"Seriously, how did you know I was in trouble?"

"I just did, Emme!" His ragged breathing hinted at words carefully weighed, measured, and left unsaid, but the potency of the ones he spoke battered me.

"So, where is your buddy? What did y'all do after you left the club? Why did he leave you hangin'?"

"You saw us at the club?"

"I *felt* you at first. And then I felt him, something I didn't care for. At all. After that I couldn't get good reception on channel Emme Vaughn. You were in and out, and then you were out. Why do you think that was?"

"I don't know."

He sighed, then raked his fingers through his shiny blacktino hair. "I'm worried here, Emme. Have you been making indelible connections with yo' boy? Because since that first day in Denny's, I've thought *our* connection was unforgettable. I was inside your soul, and you were inside mine. So what's up with Jean-Paul?"

"I don't know."

"You don't know? Well maybe you can explain why his scent is all over you."

"Is it?"

"I'm guessing that's his cologne you reek of, unless you've made even more friends today."

"That wasn't cool of you to say, Francesco."

"I'm thinking a lot is not cool tonight. I'm going

to ask you again. Anything you need to tell me, baby? Because now would be the time."

"The only thing I have to say is that I really don't know what's going on with me, and I love you with all my heart, even if some chick did put her drawers in your pocket."

"I have to give my female fans the illusion that I'm into each and every one of them the way I'm into you. That sells jazz."

"You have too much talent for me to buy that, Francis."

"I've had talent all my life, but in order to work a club, I have to be a musician *and* an entertainer. I put that drunken skank's unmentionables in the trash along with her phone number as soon as I left the stage. Did you kiss him?"

"No."

"How did his cologne get on you like that?"

"At church. He took me to St. Augustine's."

"That must have been some heckuva peace y'all passed." He practically hissed the words.

"I'm sorry," I said, my head pounding so badly it was hard to see straight.

"How could you, Emme?"

"It isn't what you think."

"Did he drug you or something? I don't under-stand! You were on the street, with this dude's energy! Help me figure out what you're doing here."

"I wish I knew."

He paced the floor. "Are you attracted to him?"

"He's very attractive, and I am kinda drawn to him, but I'm a little confused right now."

"You're confused?"

"I'm sorry. Things are really fuzzy."

"Did he . . ." He seemed to struggle for the right words. "Did he *do* anything to you that you might be afraid, or ashamed, to tell me about? Did he hurt you? You know what I'm asking you, right?"

"No. I mean, yes, I know what you're asking, and no, he didn't do anything."

"So whatever happened, you wanted it to happen?"

"I'm confused. I'm sorry."

My consciousness was flickering, and I closed my eyes to keep the room from spinning. Speaking had taken far too much effort.

Francis huffed, as angry as I'd ever seen him. "What am I supposed to do with this? Huh?"

"I think you're supposed to forgive me, because I know not what I'm doing."

"You know not what you're doing? You've twisted the words of Jesus. Tell me, Emme, who's about to be crucified here? Me?"

And then I was gone. Whatever he said after that, I couldn't tell you.

Chapter Twenty-two

I don't know how long I slept, but when I woke up, I felt better. My headache had dulled to a pulse-like throb against my temples, but I was so hungry it felt like my stomach was touching my back. I could smell Miss Marie's cooking downstairs and my insides jumped in anticipation.

I reached for Francis, but he wasn't beside me anymore. My mama was. She was sitting on the edge of the bed watching television. *The Dr. Oz Show.*

"Mama?"

"Good afternoon, baby. You know, watching Dr. Oz is like going to medical school."

"Where is Francis?"

"I need to reduce my sugar intake. Apparently it wreaks havoc with a woman of a certain age's hormones."

"Francesco," I called out. No answer.

That's when I saw the paper folded on the pillow beside me. I almost left it there. Just almost leapt out of the bed, asked my mama if she would like to accompany me downstairs for some of Miss Marie's incredible breakfast, and got on with whatever the rest of my raggedy life had in store. My heart was already broken, though I had to admit, a letter telling me he had left would truly be poetic justice.

I felt for my engagement ring. He hadn't slipped it off my finger while I slept. That was a good sign, or so I hoped. Maybe he just needed time. But somehow I knew it wasn't that.

"Did you read it, Mama?"

She stared at the television screen. "Well, now I know how hiccuping works. I can't imagine what I'll do with that information, but it's good to know. Maybe it'll surprise me and come in handy one day."

"Mommy?" I croaked.

"We can just go home, baby. I can take you to the store and get you some clothes that aren't black, and we can go to the salon and get our hair done. Jean-Paul seems smitten with you, and maybe you should think about what the two of you can have together. After some time has passed, of course."

"Francis is my destiny."

"You're young, Emme. You don't know what your destiny is. Jean-Paul can—"

"Bump it!" I snatched the paper and unfolded it. Mama didn't try to stop me. Francis had found a typewriter somewhere, and rows of neat letters, double-spaced, filled the page:

Emme,

Sometime after you had fallen asleep I had an epiphany. It came to me that I couldn't feel you like I had been because whatever happened between you and Jean-Paul damaged our connection.

How did this happen? He hasn't spent time with you like I have. He hasn't taken care of you, or made sure you had everything you needed, or loved you like I do. His ring isn't on your finger. You don't know how hard

I had to work to secure those things for you. You will never know. But of course, we vibed like that the first night we met, too. It stands to reason that such a thing could happen again, and what we shared must not be as special as I thought it was. I feel like a real sucker.

It's funny, I expected you to run from me, and you didn't disappoint. You left a brotha twice! But I would never have guessed you'd ~~cheat on~~ betray me.

I don't know why you came to me last night ~~after you left him~~. I'm not even sure you know why, and since you can't give me any answers, and you've stomped all over my heart in the diva boots that *I* bought you, I'll make it easy for you and free you to pursue whatever destiny you have with him without getting in your way.

I guess Jane Doe was wrong about us, and that's too bad, because I believed it. Now nothing seems sound, and I don't trust anything in this world anymore.

Have a nice life, Emme. Despite my anger, I hope you ~~and Jean-Paul~~ find some happiness.

NO! STAY AWAY FROM JEAN-PAUL!!! I've said this so many times, but it's true: I don't have to be a sensitive to know some things. He ain't good for you. Something ain't right about him. Trust!

Frank

P.S. Sell the ring. Give the money to the poor. It's what Saint Clare would do.

I folded the letter, placed it on the pillow where I'd found it, and cried in my mama's arms.

Chapter Twenty-three

For six days God worked, and on the seventh day he rested. I am not God. For six days I rested, and on the seventh day, I dragged my carcass out of bed because someone said I needed to get to work.

When I say I rested, I mean exactly that. I slept like the dead more hours than I was awake. It was the only thing that kept me from bawling. Sometimes, I cried until I fell asleep. The highlight of my days that dismal week was watching *The Dr. Oz Show* with Mama. She was right. Watching it was a real education. In that short span of time I learned how to spot the painful warning signs of lung, colon, and ovarian cancer, how to lose two hundred and fifty pounds without surgery, and the importance of sleep, which proved to be vital information. I did not, however, find out how to heal the malady afflicting me.

On the first day, Jean-Paul came to me. I refused to see him, and we repeated this dance on the second and third day. He skipped the fourth and fifth and came back the sixth. That Friday night he refused to take no for an answer. I wondered what had taken him so long to revert to his usual modus operandi and manipulate his way into my life, whether I wanted him there or not.

He found me in bed, the television watching me. Like a sleek black panther he skulked into the room. I was surprised that something in me was glad to see him.

"*Lève-toi, ma fille.*" He was cross with me.

"Anybody tell you I don't speak French?"

"I said get up."

"All that was just two words in English? I'm beginning to think your translations are not altogether honest."

"*Lève-toi, ma chérie.*"

"Okay. I get it. This is like some kind of language

immersion thing that I have no interest in, right? Not that my lack of interest ever stopped you. But if it makes you feel better I do know *ma chérie* means 'my dear.' At least I think so. Which leads to the question: what did you call me before after you said 'get up' in French the first time?"

"I will drag you out of that bed, Emme."

I stretched, as languid as a cat. "Why?"

"Because you are being a silly girl."

"So what? You know what they say: it's never too late to have a happy childhood."

He took me by the arm. "You stink. And it doesn't appear that you've combed your hair in days. I am hoping I am wrong about you brushing your teeth."

I blew a long breath of funk in his face, which he waved away.

"I was right," he said hoisting me to my feet. "Come."

"Where?"

"To the shower."

"I'll take a shower tomorrow." But we were already on the way, Jean-Paul having taken the lead in this affair. I noticed my mama and her husband sat idly by and allowed this mistreatment.

"Y'all ain't right," I muttered, before he thrust me into the bathroom.

There we stood in the cramped space, in front of the mirror where he had held my face in his hands and healed.

I don't know how I avoided seeing myself for all those days, but the white-haired, haggard, hollow-cheeked girl I saw shocked me. I've seen demon-possessed people who looked better.

"Which one is your toothbrush?" Jean-Paul asked.

"Purple," I murmured, embarrassed, as my sorrow gave way to shame. Jean-Paul thrust my toothbrush in my hand. He didn't have to give me directions. I handled my business while he watched, offering no recriminations. When I was done, in front of that same mirror, he took a comb and ran it through my tangle of hair. The gesture was so full of tenderness tears welled in my eyes.

"*Ne pleure pas, ma petite,*" he said, his voice as soothing as a lullaby. I figured that was somewhere on the spectrum of "don't cry." And something about being little, which was exactly how I felt.

He set the comb on the sink and smoothed my hair with his hands. A shake of his head exposed his pity. Jean-Paul cradled my face in his hands as he had before, wiping tears instead of spots from my face. There was no supernatural heat emanating from his hands. The warmth I felt was his compassion.

"Can you heal my heart?"

"*Non.*"

"Why did I do that, Jean-Paul? Why did I mess up everything?"

"There is no need to discuss this now."

"All I had to do was tell him there was nothing between us."

"That would have been a lie, *ma petite.*" I didn't argue. He'd spoken the truth.

"Take a shower, and then we will go out."

I nodded, and he pulled me into his embrace. His breath felt warm as he spoke into my hair, and I felt as if he were sowing his words like seed into the hungry, welcoming ground that was my mind.

"You will hurt, and think of nothing but him for the entire night, but you will dance anyway, laugh, and have strong drink. And tomorrow you will wake up, thinking of nothing but him. Do not turn on the television. Pretend you are alive, giving no regard to how you feel. Work. Repeat the formula. The day will come when you will look into this mirror and be enchanted by the beautiful, snowy-haired stranger before you. You will greet her thinking it is love at first sight. With immense joy you will say, '*Mademoiselle*, I am delighted to meet you.' And the beautiful stranger will say to you, 'I have loved you all along.'"

He kissed me on the top of my head, reluctantly released me, and turned on the shower. "I will send Mama Abby in with clothing. Take your time."

I didn't feel anything but the cavernous hole Francis had left in my soul, but I cast my dirty clothes off like weights and stepped into the shower, letting the water mingle with my tears. I keened and howled like an animal, begging God to wash the away my grief. Then I picked up the soap, scrubbed my body clean, and pretended to be alive.

Chapter Twenty-four

I expected my mother to place my uniform of black jeans and baby-doll T-shirt, along with black cotton camisole and boy shorts, on the bathroom counter. What I found hanging on the door had to be one of Audrey Hepburn's little red dresses. A jaunty red bow circled the bodice of the silk strapless dress. It would reveal the marks on my chest but people would think I had some artsy tattoo thing going on, and I wouldn't let that bother me. Not in this dress. The A-line skirt would accentuate my long legs and other notable assets, and the satin peep-toe stilettos would ensure Emme Vaughn towered over mere mortals.

Too bad my hair still looked like a nest. I was just going to try a ponytail, and offered up a quick prayer that the fashion police wouldn't call me to the carpet about it, but when I came out of the bathroom Mama met me, blow dryer in one hand, hot comb in the other. No flatironing for her. She was old school. Before Jean-Paul could catch a glimpse of me, she had my long pale locks dried, pressed bone straight, and twisted into a chic updo. I put my face on myself, with makeup Francis purchased, except for the eyeliner and false eyelashes. Those came from Mama, though I'd never seen her wearing such things. I guessed marriage agreed with her, and I was sorry I had clowned on her the way I did.

After a lot of fussing and fawning over me, my mother regarded me with tears misting her eyes. She was kind enough to not comment about the marks so clearly visible. Mama dealt with enough devils to let me keep my dignity.

"I guess you get to be the princess at the ball after all." She handed me a black wrap. "Let's go see your prince," she said. I didn't tell her my prince was gone, and I feared I'd never see him again.

But I'd try what Jean-Paul asked me to: go out,

dance, laugh. He'd obviously paid a pretty penny for my gear. It wasn't too late to learn gratefulness. God would still accept my meager offerings.

When I walked into the parlor, Jack and Jean-Paul stood. Jean-Paul may not have been my prince, but he looked like somebody's. He'd changed from his crisp, dark jeans and camel turtleneck into a black tuxedo with a red satin tie. He was gonna make some poor woman very happy, and completely miserable one day. Better her than me.

I think Jack's papa heart stuck his chest out. "You look good, Em." I didn't tell him only my mama calls me that.

"Thank you, Papa Jack."

He gave a quick nod and turned his face away. I think I'd touched his heart, and how stinkin' easy was that to do?

Jean-Paul never took his eyes off me, until he swept me into a delicate embrace. He whispered in my ear, *"Tu es élégante, et parfait en tous points. Je suis stupéfait par vos soins de beauté."*

"I heard that," Jack teased.

"Yes, but did you understand him?" I said. "Because I didn't."

Jack beamed. "He said you're perfect."

I laughed. "Uhn huh. Why do I have a feeling that isn't all he said?"

"Maybe it wasn't. You'll have to figure out the rest for yourself."

Jean-Paul held out his arm and I took it and let him escort me out the door while my parents waved us away. I pondered his maddening French. What kinds of things does he say that are lost to me in his translations? He'd said more than I was perfect, something no one, including Francesco, had ever said about me. And he, too, could see the bizarre markings on me. All I could gather is that Jean-Paul whispered something about beauty to me. Whatever it was, I'd drop it in the vast, yawning emptiness inside me. I hoped I'd be able to retrieve it when needed.

Chapter Twenty-five

As soon we said good-bye to my folks and closed the door behind us Jean-Paul stopped me.

"Tonight, I want you to let yourself feel."

The night air prickled my skin, but I didn't think he meant that. "I thought you said my job was to pretend to be alive. I don't want to feel."

"I'm not talking about these ponderous emotions absorbing you now, Emme. I want you to give yourself over to sensual pleasure."

I drew my shoulders back. "Uhhhh . . . Exactly where are we going?"

My serious question triggered his wide smile. "We are going dancing, *ma pauvre chérie*, but our indulgences have already begun. You are wearing an exquisite dress of the finest silk. I want you to touch yourself."

"Now you're trippin.' I'm going back inside."

"I'm serious."

"I know, which is why I'm going back in the house. That sounds nasty, Jean-Paul."

"Of course it does. To you. You've disconnected from your body; it's an understandable response to having been sexually assaulted. But you shouldn't punish your body. Your body did nothing to harm you. Nor did it do anything to cause the abuse. So stop punishing it."

I opened my mouth to say something but he stopped me, pressing his finger to my lips.

"Despite your unconvincing mental assent, you are punishing your body. You dress like a twelve-year-old, but you won't allow yourself the color a prepubescent girl would. You don't permit yourself be touched without experiencing intense emotional discomfort or self-doubt. It is only when you are deeply distressed that you bypass your body's censors and feel deep pleasure."

I didn't implicate myself any further.

"What did you and Francis do when you were together?"

"It's getting cold out here, Jean-Paul, and one of us is bare-legged."

"Tell me. What did you do to have fun?"

I tugged Mama's wrap tighter around me. "You don't have to do anything bad to have fun."

"I never said you had to do something you believe is immoral to have fun. I simply asked what you did to have fun. Did you go bowling? Or to the movies? Did you sit at home on the couch for hours watching television and cuddling." He gave me a knowing glance. "Emme, have you ever cuddled anyone other than your mother?"

I swallowed. "Francis and I went out to dinner together, and church." I could probably count the number of times on my fingers. "We spent time with each other." Until a demon attack freaked me out and his godmother wouldn't allow us to be alone. "We talked." Mostly him, as he educated me in what I jokingly called demon school. "We would kiss." Until I ran away. Twice.

"You've never actually had fun with him, have you?"

"We loved each other. I still love him."

"I'm certain you do, but there was no way you

were about to marry him, I don't care what you told yourself. You sabotaged your relationship, allowing him to believe we were involved in a way we weren't."

"I was sick that night; confused."

"But you knew what he was thinking. You hid behind this notion of being overwhelmed, and indeed you were, but it would have only taken a few moments to explain."

"It would have complicated things."

"He is a sensitive himself. He experienced exactly what you did. The headaches, the anxiety, the panic."

I grabbed my head. "I can't believe I didn't put this together. He went though this same thing, at the same age, right before he met his father. He thought it was panic attacks he was having."

"You gave him his walking papers, and both of you knew it. He left because you weren't ready. Oh, I'm certain the thought of me was a distraction, but he really left because from his arrival at your parents' house, until the time he wrote you that letter, you showed him in a number of ways that you can't handle him."

I fixed my gaze on my stilettos, but he took my chin between his thumb and forefinger and lifted my head. "You are driven by false guilt. It's because you're unaware of your essential innocence."

"I'm not innocent."

"See! You've proven my point." He loosened the wrap covering my shoulders and torso. "Feel the silk on your body."

"I don't want to."

"Do you need me to show you how? I can demonstrate this action if you'd rather I slide my hands up and down your contours. I like the feel of silk very much."

"Go ahead, if you won't be needing your hands anymore. 'Cause yo', if you do that, you'll lose 'em."

"This is very intriguing. You are aggressive now; threatening."

"You're talking about feeling me up."

"I asked, very politely, if you needed me to show you how to do something a newborn baby would do naturally, without a whit of guilt, for the sheer delight of it."

He took my hand in his, and pressed my palm against the lustrous fabric covering my stomach. "I'm not asking you to commit a mortal sin. I'm asking you to relish the softness against your skin. I'm asking you to get out of you head, out of your emotions, and lose yourself in a bodily pleasure."

He moved his hand away, but mine remained in place. The silk really was incredible. And what was wrong with enjoying it? I took a deep breath and tried to concentrate every bit of awareness I had on the nerve endings in my hand.

The sublime silkiness and the cool of the night began to enliven me. I felt as if for years my body had slept, and Jean-Paul's insistence had nudged it awake, but I didn't know what I should think while I did this bizarre, freeing exercise.

"Don't think," he said. "Experience. Tonight we will be animals: guiltless, free of neurosis, bodies. We will engage all of our senses: seeing, hearing, smelling, tasting, and, *ma chérie*, touching. We will have fun! *Oui?*"

I couldn't think of a single instance, since I was a small child, of truly having a boisterous good time. I was so nervous at the prospect, my legs trembled and my stomach churned, but I had nothing to lose.

I sighed and told him, *"Oui."*

Chapter Twenty-six

I should have known something was up when Jean-Paul and I strolled outside and his car was parked in front of the house. This was not a beat-up Toyota Camry. He drove a black, newer model Mercedes, as clean as a germophobe's hands. How in the heck could a twenty-five-year-old afford that kind of whip?

"I'm a broker."

I don't even know why I was surprised. "Dude, is

there, like, a hole in my head that allows people to peek at my thoughts?"

"How many people do you think are reading your thoughts, Emme?" He opened the door to the carriage and settled the princess inside.

"Well, there's you; Francis can do it; Jane Doe."

"What do the three of us have in common?" He even got into the car with a flourish, before he buckled his seatbelt.

I hesitated to click on mine, reveling in the smooth silk dress a little too much, but he gave me a look that told me safety wasn't optional, so I buckled up too.

"All three of you are sensitives?"

"Yes, but it isn't that simple. Perhaps the commonality is that the three of us are more mindful than you are currently."

"Mindful? Are you serious?"

"Emme, even without using your striking gifts, observing people carefully can tell you much more than you may wish to know about them. Being like the Australian man on *The Mentalist* is not difficult at all. But if, by means of the Spirit, you are tapping into the thoughts and feelings of others, you are practicing awareness beyond the ordinary. You paying attention deeply to Spirit in your spirit, to what is right in front of you, and to what is inside of you: God. How does God most often speak to you, Emme?"

"The Bible says he speaks as a still, small voice."

"I didn't ask you what the Bible says, *ma chérie*, I know what the Bible says. I have a master's degree in black Catholic studies from Xavier. I am asking you about a very personal experience. How does God most often speak to you?"

His questions took me aback. It was hard to get a handle on him. "A lot of crazy things happen. I mean, you know a demon tried to make me look like a spotted owl."

"It's a very simple question."

"I hear him inside me. Like he has this little house and it's deep down in my core. And I know it's him. I mean, he isn't always chatty, but when he speaks, I hear it." I nodded, thinking that yes, this was the absolute truth. And I was very fortunate that God lived in a little house inside me.

"When you visit that house where God lives more often, you will sharpen your gift. Saint Teresa of Avila called her house an interior castle, made of a diamond. And in it were many dwellings, millions of them, and one of the dwellings in the castle was self-knowledge. Do not worry; God never leaves the castle. You're always close to him in there. The longer you stay in that room, the more you will see that human beings are essentially beset by the same urges and hungers. We enjoy the same pleasures and resist the same pains. This is the foundation of knowing what others are thinking. Soon all you will need is a simple prompt, and you will know the hearts of men."

"So, you think I'll be able to read your thoughts someday?"

"But of course, I'm counting on it."

∾

Before I knew it we were on the outskirts of the city and had pulled up to a spectacular plantation house.

"Who lives here?" I asked. I felt so out of my league.

"A client."

"What kind of broker did you say you were?"

He smiled, but it lacked the warmth of most of his grins. "I didn't say."

I figured this was a good time to go to that little house, have a chat with God, and watch for prompts to help me see what was right in front of my face.

∾

I was about to attend a heckuva soiree. This was no ghetto, dollar-a-head house party. Jean-Paul's client had valet parking. The house itself was a ginormous antebellum number: four stories, a dozen or more columns, and galleries on three façades. It was circled by the austere splendor of a veritable forest, and in the center was a garden that must have been mind-blowing in the summer. At the entrance Jean-Paul warned me, "This is a feast for your eyes, and inside is no less grandiose, but make no mistake, we are about to enter a den of debauchery. Have fun!" He winked at me and reached for the doorbell.

I grabbed his hand. "Wait."

"What is it, *ma chérie?*"

"The last time I was out, all this stuff hit me. I don't want to be in there with my head banging, trying to keep vomit from splattering all over the silken goodness I'm rockin'."

"Stay close to me. If you are overwhelmed, I will know, and we'll make adjustments, but I suspect you won't have as much of a problem as before. You have been asleep for five days, and I'll daresay your abilities have receded to mere inner background noise. But tonight, we are only bodies, and there will be none of that discerning spirits, *très bien?*"

I wasn't crazy about discerning spirits anyway, especially when it was virtually unrelenting. "Okay. *Très bien?*" I smiled at him this time.

He laughed, "See, you are already speaking my language."

~

A beautiful woman, stacked like pancakes on a grand-slam breakfast, answered the door and ushered us inside. She wore red, but her dress wasn't nearly as fly as mine. Neither were her shoes. She led us through the most opulent foyer I'd ever seen and up a staircase leading to the third floor.

If I was just a body, I was a confused one. Three of my senses—seeing, smelling, and feeling—were assaulted by the most ridiculously swanky digs ever. The place had a *sick* sound system bumping out bass that reverberated through me. The fragrance of a profusion of fresh-cut flowers mingled with the odors of sweat, booze, weed, and expensive incense, and a musky smell permeated the place that I didn't even want to know the origin of.

All the men wore black tuxedos, and the women wore red. Most of them had far less fabric than the classy dress I wore; a couple of chicks were sporting what amounted to embroidery floss. Those cows kinda hurt a sistah's eyes, but not Jean-Paul's. He took them in with gusto, and I wasn't the least bit jealous. I didn't think about it, and that freed me from judging him, or anyone else. But I did have a question.

"Why is everybody dressed like this?"

"It's a red party. The host always has a theme. It could be anything. He is . . . ridiculous. Not that I mind tonight's theme; you look ravishing decked in crimson."

I couldn't help but tease him. "Apropos, since you've brought me to Dante's Inferno."

He tossed his head back and laughed, and I could tell his mood had grown more expansive. "I'm afraid you'll only find three circles of his vision of hell here."

"Which three would those be?"

"The second, third, and fourth: lust, gluttony, and greed."

"What?" I said, buoyed by the sensuous music filling me. "No sixth circle for heretics here?"

"If there is, we won't know. We'll be too busy dancing to argue theology."

He tried to pull me to the dance floor, but I had a confession. "Wait a minute, Jean-Paul."

He let out an exaggerated sigh. "Are you thinking? I told you not to think."

"I'm not thinking. It's just . . . I don't know how to dance that good."

He burst out laughing. "*Viens ici*, woman! I will teach you."

As if on cue a zydeco tune as scorching as Louisiana hot pepper sauce boomed through the speakers, and Jean-Paul drew me close to him. "Remember: don't think. Let the music move you. We'll start with this two-step, and then follow me."

I was grateful that the two-step didn't involve the bumping and grinding going on around me. His free-flowing moves became increasing complicated, but I kept up, until he and I had ripped up the dance floor enough to draw a crowd of cheering spectators. I can't remember when I laughed so much, though really, it was a hollow sound. I never lost sight of the paradox I was living. It's true, I was mostly giving myself to the pleasures of the body. Yet Jean-Paul was right. I thought only of Francis the entire night. But the music dulled my anguish.

After we danced ourselves silly, he took me to another level of the house where a feast was laid out that made Miss Marie's breakfast look like a soup kitchen. I was glad we did all that dancing, because I'd worked up a ravenous hunger. I'd planned on having more than my share of calories.

Jean-Paul and I kinda grazed, moving from finger foods to more luxurious fare like rock lobster, but we stuck close to the table, preferring to stand and people-watch instead of sit down and get our eat on.

I noticed a man staring at us. Dude was *big*. Ordinarily I wouldn't have thought much about his size. My friend, Kiki, who offered me refuge while I was hiding from the system, weighed over five hundred pounds, but she didn't look at me like I was a tender roast. And Big Boy looked hungry.

I nodded toward the man. "Who's two tons of fun over there staring at me?"

"That's my client. He owns this house, he's the devil in this den, and he takes great pleasure in his role."

"What do you do for him?"

"I've already told you: I'm his broker. I procure commodities on his behalf. You would not believe his appetites."

"I think I would."

I wanted to get out of there. The man looked too hungry, like he was greed personified. Unfortunately, I didn't let my discomfort be known to Jean-Paul fast enough. Jabba the Hutt tottered over to us, consuming me with his eyes.

He greeted Jean-Paul with a drunken drawl, "Daaaaaarlin'." No handshake. He didn't even look at him. "Who is this delectable creature?" He slurred "who is" so that it sounded like a single word. "I swear she is a vision in red."

Up close, dude was behemoth, as wide as he was tall. And he was tall, longer than Jean-Paul, but two hundred and fifty pounds heavier. I wondered if he watched *The Dr. Oz Show.* He could help him with that.

Turning the charm on thick, Jean-Paul said, "This is my half-sister, Emme. She just came to town from Michigan." He strained to smile. "Emme, this is Boko. I've already riveted you with tales about him."

A bellowing laugh poured out of Boko's mouth. "Are you having a good time, Angie?" he said, leering at me. He kept his gaze on my chest but said nothing about the markings.

I didn't even bother to correct him. I didn't want that freak to remember my name. I shot a look at Jean-Paul before answering. "I've had a great time."

Now he gave his full attention to Jean-Paul, flopping his ham-hock hand on his shoulder. "Well done, my boy. You bring Angie back to see me, ya hear?" He simpered like he knew Jean-Paul would do just that.

"I'd be delighted to."

"Come on back and see me tomorrow." He said tomorrow like "tamara." "I don't want to mix business with . . ." His gaze swept over me, lingering at my breasts. "Pleasure." Again, he drew out so it sounded like "pleashaaaaa."

Then he lumbered away.

"Why did you introduce me to that fool?"

"I wanted to see what you thought of him. He is truly diabolically possessed."

"Diabolically possessed people love their demons," I said. "They become their demons. They don't want to be free."

"Hell would reject him."

"It's true. Dude, that is the grossest person I've ever met. And keep in mind I'm an exorcist." I thought he'd get a laugh out of that, but he only looked after Boko, muttering a stream of obscenities.

"Does he owe you money or something? You sure are hard on him."

"He owes me more than that."

"Why do you work for him?"

His eyes had the hardest glint I'd seen in Jean-Paul since we'd met. "I am a damned ambitious man."

I knew I wasn't supposed to be thinking, but I found "damned ambitious" a curious choice of words for a man who always said exactly what he meant. I tucked that away also, to ponder when I had an occasion to think.

Chapter Twenty-seven

I woke up telling heartache good morning, like I was Billie Holiday. I thought of nothing but Francis. However, I did take Jean-Paul's advice: I did not turn on the television. Dr. Oz would have to soldier on without me.

On the seventh day I worked. My first task was to fortify the house. After the last episode we had had no more trouble. Demons don't usually go easy, but I was hoping the Lord would hold them at bay until I got myself together. Despite my unhappiness, I felt a sprout of hope. I believed one day it would bud, then flower. For now: pretend to be alive.

Again, I wished Francis were around, with his crazy portable exorcism kit and library of memorized warfare prayers. All I had left were a few he'd printed out that I'd tucked in the breviary Jane Doe gave me, along with some she'd written in the margins.

Mama was in the kitchen drinking coffee. The sunshine-yellow room reminded me, with a stab of pain, of our life before she was riddled with demons. It was odd how little things made me ache. But it was high time I stopped acting like a stupid kid. Despite myself, I felt like I was slowly growing into those big-girl panties Ms. Mary told me to put on.

I kissed Mama on the top of her head. I didn't feel like it, but I was consciously practicing touching like a normal person: fake it till you make it.

"Good morning, baby!"

"Hey, Mama. Any more coffee?"

"It's brewing. I'll get you a cup."

"Nope. You sit right there. I'll get it myself."

She gave me a sly smile. "You must have had a good night."

"It was pretty amazing. Jean-Paul taught me how to zydeco dance."

"Did he?"

"I'm about to do some housecleaning."

Mama glanced around, confused. "You think my homemaking skills are off?" She looked genuinely concerned.

"Mama, the house looks fine. I need to bless it, and ask God to protect us from evil."

She circled her fingers around the rim of her coffee mug and thought for a moment. "Is there anything I can do to help?"

"Are you sure? You looked really upset the other day."

"I was, Emme, and then you flashed into my mind. You faced those demons with as much courage as I saw in Jane Doe. You inspired me." She shook her head, regarding me with a crooked smile. "I failed you. I also failed myself. Sometimes I wonder if I had handled the whole thing differently, would we have had an entirely different outcome? Perhaps if I had dealt with the rape with more courage and . . ." She hesitated. "And 'badditude' like my child has, neither of us would have suffered so much."

"Okay, did you just say 'badditude'?" Her fair skin blushed. I got up and hugged her. "It's all good, Mama. You kept me, even though most women would have aborted me, or put me up for adoption. You loved me so much I didn't know my father raped you. I think you did the best you could." I thought about my Maria Goretti icon, sitting on the night-stand in what was now my very own bedroom. "We tried."

I took a gulp of coffee and purposely tried to correct my grammar to show Mama I had mad love for her saying "badditude" just for me. "I have to go run a few errands. I'll need a few sacramentals for the housecleaning. Would you happen to know where any local Benedictines are?"

"You can try the phone book. It's in the parlor on the telephone table."

I pretended to be alive and sauntered into the parlor, when a slow trudge would do for all my walking needs. The Yellow Pages were under the cherry-wood telephone table just as she said. I hardly knew anyone with a landline, much less a telephone table to go with it. Mama had organized the space Martha Stewart neat, complete with a pen and message pad. I have no idea why I suddenly became so nosy, but I picked up the pad and thumbed through the last few messages.

Francis's name and phone number were scrawled on a page from the day he left me. I could imagine that scene: Francis calling, trying to explain what remained a mystery to him. Mama coming because I was sick, knowing he'd leave and shatter my heart. I tore the paper out of the pad, fingered the letters and numbers, then placed my hand on the phone. I waited; picked up the receiver and held it to my ear; then set it down on the cradle. He probably spit on the ground every time he thought of me, which probably wasn't much.

I sighed. "I'm so sorry, Francesco."

Then I grabbed the Yellow Pages and went to handle my business.

～

I totally couldn't find a community of Benedictines nearby. I was in the most Catholic freakin' place in America, and there was not a community of my favorite monks to be seen. The benefit of being in such a ridiculously Catholic city was that it wasn't hard to find a Catholic bookstore. I couldn't walk to it, but I had no qualms about jumping on a bus. It was mostly a straight shot down South Carrollton, and if my estimation was correct, I'd be back in Tremé in no time.

True to form, I thought of nothing but Francis. Riding through his beloved NOLA filled me with melancholy. Alone, I didn't have to do as much pretending. I slogged off the bus with my shoulders rounded and went through the store without cracking open a single book. I bought a few dozen Saint Benedict jubilee medals and three holy water bottles. Before I went back to the house, I stopped at St. Augustine's, hoping the parish priest was hanging around in the church or rectory and could give a sistah some blessings.

A few people were in the building. The custodian, who was in the sanctuary cleaning that Saturday morning for Sunday's Mass, let me in. He was a kindly old Latino man, or maybe he was Creole. I hadn't quite figured out the ethnic gumbo that was NOLA yet. I just loved it, and hoped it would soon love me.

I asked if I could sit and talk to Jesus for a few minutes, and he obliged me. This time I thought of not only of Francis, but of Jean-Paul too, and his wonderful stories. I sat on one of the slave pews, and in the quiet, did a little business with God.

"Lord, Jean-Paul was totally right about me. I've been disconnected. Not just from my body, but from love. I tried to love, but I kept failing. Something in me is broke, and I don't know how to fix it. That broken thing keep hurting Francis, and I am so sorry about that."

My voice broke, and my own grief poured out of me in tears. Spontaneous words to pray disappeared, so I fell back on the familiar words of the act of contrition. Who says just because you memorized a prayer it's vain repetition?

"O my God, I am heartily sorry for having offended thee. I detest all of my sins because of your just punishments, but most of all because they offend you, my God, who are all-good and deserving of all my love. I firmly resolve, with the help of your grace, to sin no more and avoid the near occasions of sin." I choked before I could say "amen."

Someone's hand touched my shoulder, and I thought this was no time to see the freakin' dead. I turned to find a priest offering me tissues and a heaping portion of compassion. He was a handsome young man, with a shining bald head and a luminous smile, who didn't appear to be a whole lot older than Jean-Paul. His voice was Southern, spiced with Creole. "I'm Father Norman. Can I help you?"

"I'm Emme, and I'm a big ol' sinner."

"Would you like me to hear your confession?"

I nodded, and he blessed me, then let me unburden my heart to Jesus. I told him everything, even stuff I hadn't thought of since I was back in Inkster. I might not have cheated on Francis, but I certainly had betrayed him because of my own fears, which was selfish. As penance Father Norman asked two things of me: that I would remember that the blood of Christ cleanses us from every stain, and that includes the stains other people taint you with.

And to talk to Francis, and ask his forgiveness for the things I'd done to him. The caveat was I had to do it face to face.

I left St. Augustine's with my sins forgiven and a heckuva task before me. Oh, and a few dozen *blessed* Saint Benedict medals, three bottles full of holy water, and some regular table salt, now made holy by the prayers of a man of God. It was time to work it now, Exorsistah style.

∾

Back at the house, Mama and I got ready to clean. We went through every room, though she was concerned about the sacramentals. She so wasn't Catholic.

"Mama, it's not superstitious. This isn't hocus-pocus or some kind of magic. It's prayer. It's like when you light a candle at church. That's a prayer. It'll keep on flickering its light to heaven, illuminating God's throne with your sincerest intentions and petitions. Same thing with Saint Benedict medals. Mama, Saint Benedict was a heckuva—I mean a fine exorcist. When I'm wearing my Jubilee medal, I'm continually asking that blessed man of God, who has joined the great cloud of witnesses, to remember me to the Christ he loved."

"I don't know about this, Emme. I want to trust you, but . . ."

I waited, but she never said what her issue was.

"Mama, I don't want you to trust me. I want you to put every iota of faith you have in God. If God does not infuse these things with grace, they're just trinkets anyway. Maybe they'll make you feel a little better, like any superstitious thing you do would, but they won't effect any change in your life. But if God really is kind enough to give us a little more of his protection this way, and I happen to know he is, well, I want to go with that care."

She nodded, and I kept sweeping the house with prayers, placing medals in every room and burying them all around the perimeter of the house. I sprinkled the blessed salt in the corners, doused the walls, floors, and ceilings with holy water, and rebuked the devil. I hung my icon of Maria Goretti in the spot that devil messed up. Papa Jack had repainted the wall and it was now, ironically, haint blue. I didn't know if my mama knew what was up with that color, but I wouldn't put it past Papa Jack to have known, doing what he felt he had to do. Most of all I prayed that God would put a hedge around us like he did Job.

May the demons and devils stay out, and the angels and love stay in. Amen.

Chapter Twenty-eight

No sooner had we said the last prayer and sat on the sofa, tired from the exertion it takes to do all that rebuking and blessing, than Papa Jack surprised us with a Christmas tree and all the trimmings.

Mama lit up like the lights Bourbon Street.

"I haven't had a Christmas tree since . . ."

When her words trailed off I knew she was looking at me, but I had become an adept pretender in the last few days, especially in the presence of others. I acted like I was absorbed in pulling ornaments out of the bag and had no idea she was about to reference the horrendous last year we had a Christmas tree. Instead I replaced my bad memory with the very recent one at the beginning of the month, when I was still at St. Benedict's Abbey. Brother Michael and I were decorating the tree when Jane Doe appeared like a whirlwind, wrecking my life for its own good.

Mama never finished what she was going to say. Papa Jack had mounted the tree in the stand and added water. I put on my perkiest voice.

"Let's get some bling on this baby." We got busy making new memories.

The radio had filled the parlor with back-to-back Michael Bublé, and we had just crooned "The Christmas Song." Well, I sang most of it. Mama and Papa Jack did a lot of smooching. I was glad to see them so happy, but I couldn't help but think about you-know-who. For the first time I wished I had my mother's courage to love and trust a man so much after she'd been raped and even possessed as a direct result of her contact with him. She had the confidence in her body that I lacked. She wasn't big on the presence of evil, but with what was most important she was fine. It was the opposite for me. I could chase a devil back to hell, but if Francis wanted to make out like my parents were, in front of someone no less, I'd have straight tripped on him. I still hadn't dredged up the courage to call him.

The second Michael Bublé song had come on, "Let It Snow," and we'd gotten to the part where he sings, "Oh the weather outside is frightful." The instant I belted out the word "frightful," tinsel in hand, guess who penetrated our freshly prayed-in hedge of protection? I should have asked God to keep dead folks out, too.

She scared the stuffing out of me, but nobody noticed my reaction but Celestine. Mama and Papa Jack were still canoodling. At least Celestine had her head on all the way. Few things can ruin the Christmas spirit more than a ghost's partially severed head flopping all over when you're trying to decorate.

What I found different was that she sat quietly on the sofa, all sad-eyed. But she stayed. I kept tossing lines of silver tinsel onto the tree, occasionally peeking behind me, and she'd still be there, looking more depressed than I felt.

An hour later I told my parents I was going to take a short walk. Jack was more leery than Mama.

"I promise I'll just go a few blocks," I assured him.

"You be careful, Em," he said. "Do you have a cell phone?"

"No."

"Abby, we're going to have to get our girl one of those iPhones."

I feigned delight. The thought of an iPhone summoned memories of Francis; we used to pray with his. And a dead girl was loitering on the sofa. It sucked to be me.

I left home fast and hot-tailed it the oracle's house. Without Jean-Paul around I was free to ask her questions I felt uncomfortable asking in his presence, especially questions about Celestine.

It took me less than ten minutes to get there, and seriously, with a dead girl on your heels you just don't worry about street crime. Ms. Mary's husband, a quiet man, opened the door, and showed me to the sitting room where she sat letting the television watch her.

"Who's there?" she said.

"It's Emme Vaughn. J-P brought me here last weekend. I got sick at the Tomb of the Unknown Slave."

"I knew it was you, *chérie*. I want to know who's the haint you're carrying with you."

∽

The three of us sat in silence in Ms. Mary Brooks's sitting room. She'd grown quiet, and I didn't know if that was her method—like, she was meditating or something—or what. After about ten everlasting minutes I cleared my throat. Ms. Mary turned her head my way.

"Do you have any advice for me?" I asked. "'Cause, seriously, I have no idea what this dead girl wants."

"She's not a very powerful spirit," Ms. Mary said. "She's not going to be able to communicate much to you."

"She sure as heck communicated her dang-gone sadness."

"No, *cher*. That was you being the sensitive you are. How long have you been seeing her?"

"Since the eleventh. She showed up as soon as we got to the welcome sign on South Claiborne."

"*Bienvenu!*" she quipped with a wave, laughing at her own joke. "Sorry. I couldn't resist. Has she done anything else?"

"That first night she kept following me, and I touched her. After that my fiancé said I'd spoken in Creole, a language I don't speak. He said I didn't even know I was doing it. Like, I was speaking in tongues, but without any awareness of it."

She humphed. "That had to be interesting."

"Depressing is more like it."

I looked at Celestine. She did not look apologetic about the suffering she had caused. "After that, I felt all these emotions that weren't mine. I could feel her regret for dying, and other things, too."

"You were chosen for this because some god has given you some potent gifts. He believed you could be trusted to help her."

"What I am supposed to do?"

"You got me, *cher*. Ghost don't come with instructions. When I help the police, I usually do it as methodically as a lead investigator would; I just happen to have on my task force God, and occasionally the saints, or other good spirits."

When she helps the police? Aw, man! She was the woman Francis mentioned who lived in Tremé and helped the cops solve murders. Ms. Mary could come in handy! I became a very loquacious young woman.

"Well, if God has done anything, he's helped me see connections. First of all, I stayed in that monastery for months before I met Miss Jane. Maybe the delay was because he knew Celestine would be killed. And then Miss Jane sent me here, and it just so happens to have coincided with my mother being well enough to have married this private investigator who knew Celestine. I started seeing Celestine right before all these gifts were recovered. It's got to mean something."

"Sounds like it to me. I'd start with asking your stepfather for as much information as you can get out of him. He's missing what you're going to see, because he doesn't have the gifts you do. You got a job?"

"Not yet."

"If he has his own agency, ask him if you can do some part-time work. Then you can be in his business and not seem nosy."

I paused.

"What is it?" Ms. Mary said. "I know you've got something. Go on and tell it."

"It's just that Miss Jane wrote me and my ex-fiancé a letter before she died, and she said me and my mama were gonna take down this evil dude, but she never said anything about Celestine. And I'm sure my fiancé is supposed to help me through this, but he broke up with me!"

Ms. Mary drummed her fingers on her ample thigh and thought for a moment. "*Cher,* here's the thing about gifts. And I don't want you to forget it. You've got your spiritual gifts: the charisms that you see used in our churches and in ministry work, things like prophecy and word of knowledge, healing and such. Charismatics are fond of those. But there are other gifts God gives, too, like the ones you and I have. They're for a different purpose. We have the ability to see spirits, whether they're angelic, demonic, or human. Sometimes we can read hearts. But no gift is foolproof. They're always subject to that slippery free will. Choices can be made that will affect the whole dynamic. So don't go writing on stone tablets like you're Moses. You just keep listening to God, paying attention to everything."

"So, the first order is to talk to my stepfather."

"No, the first order is to pray, watch, and listen. Then talk to your stepfather and repeat those first steps until you figure something out."

I looked at Celestine to see what she thought of that plan. She nodded enthusiastically, dislodging her head again, which totally grossed me out.

"You are so foul," I said to Celestine. She disappeared.

Ms. Mary laughed. "Kinda makes you wish you were blind to the spirit world like I'm blind to the natural one, don't it?"

I just nodded while she cackled at my expense.

Chapter Twenty-nine

Darkness had fallen and so I jogged home. It was a real novelty that anything felt remotely like "home." The total kookiness was that I was worried that my "dad" might be concerned about my safety. But Christmas cheer prevailed. My folks were still singing, swinging, and making merry like Christmas when I crept through the door.

"She's back!" Papa Jack announced with glee. Apparently he had imbibed a bit of eggnog, so his mood was particularly joyful. I wasn't one to miss an opportunity—unless loving Francis was part of the deal. I jumped at the chance to gauge his interest in having a new employee.

"Papa Jack?" I said. He beamed. I think he was still stoked about having a daughter who wasn't at war with him now. I hung my coat on the rack. "Do you know anyone who's hiring? Something part-time."

He rubbed his chin. "I suppose there are the usual suspects: fast food, retail. Do you have any special skills?"

I smiled. "None anybody would be interested in except paranormal science organizations. The archdiocese wouldn't even want to use me since I'm a girl and all. They tend to like their exorcists of another gender."

He got a big laugh out of that, and I do mean big.

"What about the family business?" I said. "Can you use me to do some small jobs for you? It's gotta rock being a private investigator."

Now his broad chest expanded. "Well, your mother's more interested in being a homemaker, and more clients are hiring me. If you want, I can pay you an hourly rate to look into some minor cases."

"I would so love that." I topped off my performance with an enthusiastic hug. "Thanks, Papa! Merry Christmas!"

Man, I'd be glad when I could stop pretending to be alive and actual be it.

Jean-Paul sauntered through the door with a few DVDs in his hand. The smell of his anger fouled the room, though no one else seemed to notice. He passed out hugs and kisses, and when his lips made contact with my cheek, we did that thing he and I did now. I had the distinct impression that he was doing some pretending of his own. Not just anger, but anxiety simmered behind his spirited mask, and loss greater than my own leveled him.

"What are we watching tonight?"

I nodded toward the lovebirds, leaned over to Jean-Paul, and whispered. "Probably gonna be you and me tonight, bro."

He nodded. "I'm sure you're right about that, *ma chérie.*"

It wasn't too long after Mama and Papa Jack said *bonsoir* that Jean-Paul popped a bowl of popcorn and parked on the sofa. The second-class angel Clarence was listening to the head angle Joseph's backstory about George Bailey, and I leaned against Jean-Paul's arm, with my head resting near his shoulder. Every time Jean-Paul and I hung out now, we touched. Nothing that would make me uncomfortable: just a pat here, or a friendly stroke there. Often we'd hold hands. Far from my girlfriends, and so unfamiliar with New Orleans, I had made Jean-Paul my new best friend, which is why I took the liberty of asking, "What's wrong, *camarade*?"

He didn't bother to hide his feelings. "Have you ever felt at war with yourself?"

"Yeah," I said with a snort. "It's a real problem."

"I feel like Saint Paul: I do not understand what I do. For what I want to do I do not do, but what I hate I do."

"Everybody feels that way at one time or another. Don't get down on yourself about that one."

"I'm not a devout man. I am a sinner, like Augustine before his conversion. I love women and make no pretense of chastity I neither possess nor desire. I love to drink. I am vengeful and manipulative."

"But can you be honest about yourself?" I joked. He didn't laugh at my sarcasm, and lowered his head. Now it was my turn to lift his chin.

Touching someone's face is an intimate gesture, but it wasn't nearly as hard as it would have been before. "J-P, look at me. My failed attempt at humor had some truth to it. You may be all those things, but the fact is, Augustine changed. He had someone who cared about him, storming heaven with her prayers. Shoot, I think the Catholic church made Monica a saint because through her constant petitions, one of the world's most infamous sinners became the

one of the world's most famous saints. I don't mind
being your Monica. Before you broke into your cover
of Michael Jackson's 'Bad' you said you wanted to do
right. You know what they say, dude: follow your first
mind."

He stared at the television again. "I am sorry, *ma
soeur.*"

"Did you just call me a cabbage?"

He chuckled. "Non. That is *mon chou.*" He grew
serious and looked in my eyes. "You do realize that I
love, do you not?"

I nodded. His manner was so solemn that it confused me.

"I always get what I want, Emme."

"So you said."

I turned back to the movie after that. My "I love
you, too" stayed at the tip of my tongue.

Chapter Thirty

As it got closer to Christmas, it wasn't as difficult to pretend to be alive. I had my work and a ghostly companion intent on hovering over me while I pored over her case file. Sometimes she would bang on the photos with her bloody hands. Fortunately she wasn't substantial enough to leave any stains. Papa Jack was pleased that I'd taken such a passionate interest in her case. He gave me the go-ahead to focus on it alone and paid me ten bucks an hour for the privilege!

I didn't see Jean-Paul as much. He seemed preoccupied. It bothered me, but so did what he said about getting what he wanted. He knew I was in love with Francis, and he'd never really made a move on me. Most of the time I was convinced his interest in me wasn't romantic. Then he'd make some maddening comment, leaving me unsure about what his motivations were.

Work was a welcome diversion, and on Christmas Eve, while the parents were out shopping, Celestine and I sat at the kitchen table going over her crime scene photos. By now her presence was so common I considered her as much a friend as Jean-Paul. I'd taken to talking to her. She never said anything, but at least she obliged me and figured out how to keep her head on straight.

"I've looked at these photos a thousand times, Tina. I've gone over the transcripts of these interviews. What am I missing? Maybe I should go back to Ms. Mary."

Celestine looked at me like she was saying, "Why are you so bone-headed?"

I heard a wonderfully familiar terse voice. "She's told you all you need to know, dear heart."

My head snapped up. "Miss Jane! Dude! What are you doing here?"

She looked beautiful, appearing to be about

thirty years old, her wizened earthly appearance done away with. The immortality she'd put on suited her. She wasn't as slim as she was in her last days. And her stark white dreadlocks were now cut short enough to graze her shoulders. Cute!

She took a drag of what must have been the heavenly version of a Virginia Slim. "You've interrupted my eternal joy with your inability to see what is right in front of you, Emme."

"Might I remind you that I never asked for this assignment?"

"I don't have time for your whining, dear heart," my otherworldly friend said.

"You're dead, Miss Jane. You're kinda timeless now."

"Don't be ridiculous. Having passed from death to eternal life doesn't mean I sit idly around heaven." Perfect smoke rings rose to the ceiling.

"I didn't know you could smoke in heaven."

"I'm not in heaven now, dear heart."

I sighed. She was the only person I knew who spent all her time with God and was still terse. "Did you come to tell me something about Tina?"

"I came to tell you that you must do as you've been instructed to numerous times, by Jean-Paul, and Miguel, and me, and Francis. Watch and pray, and remember, you, my dear, do not have a 'little house,' within you." She said "little house" with total contempt.

"You have an interior castle. Teresa asked me to tell you that she could find nothing on earth, or beyond it, more magnificent than the beauty and amplitude of a soul. She also asked me to say, 'Would it kill you to pick up a copy of *The Interior Castle* and read it?' Might I add she has quite an endearing accent, not unlike Miguel's, and she is, as you are wont to say, 'a whole lot of fun.'

"It would be in your best interest also to visit the room of self-knowledge. You will need the sagacity you find there."

"What does 'sagacity' mean?"

"Look it up, dear heart, and meanwhile try to infer its meaning from our conversation." She paused. "Having Jean-Paul in your life agrees with you. But he needs your help, badly."

I opened my mouth to speak but she raised a wispy finger to silence me. "The room of self-knowledge, Emme. Go there. And after that visit the inner chambers of your Beloved. Christ dwells within you, as much as he does in heaven. If you meet him in the depths of your being, you will find that all is well. I have never failed you. Good-bye, dear heart. I do not wish to see you soon."

With that she disappeared.

I sat there gaping at Tina until I could pull myself together. "Do you have any idea what she was talking about?"

She raised her hands as if to say, "Not a clue," and nodded her head toward the photos. I picked up another, trying to decipher the thing as plain as day that I couldn't figure out to save my life.

Chapter Thirty-one

The Bible passage that says "The boundary lines have fallen for me in pleasant places; I have a goodly heritage" was one of those verses I never related to until I prepared to go to midnight Mass on Christmas Eve with my family.

I wore a red velvet dress. Oh, man. I've always wanted a Christmas dress. I'd been preening in the bathroom and running my fingers across its velvety goodness—Jean-Paul really did have a lot of wisdom—when suddenly I gasped to see that I was lovely. The beautiful white-haired stranger in the mirror was me, and I loved her, body and soul.

At Mass I sat beside my Catholic-spooked mama and my thoroughly Catholic papa. On the other side was Jean-Paul, the prodigal who perplexed me, but who I loved. I had a job and a generous employer. Sure there was that occupational hazard of the dead hanging out with me, but God had restored the years the locust had eaten in a spectacular turn of events. The only thing I lacked was the person I loved most in the world.

Merry Christmas, Francis, wherever you are.

We had our *réveillon* feast at none other than Emeril Lagasse's restaurant, NOLA. *Bam!* I was going to become a fat cow in N'awlins, but I'd be a very happy bovine. First course: duck confit salad. Lord, have mercy! Second: a butternut squash bisque that surely they serve in heaven. We had buttermilk fried quail, and a warm gingerbread cake served with poached pears and cranberry chutney. That was all the Christmas gifts I needed, but over the table we exchanged the single gifts we'd give to each other.

I gave Mama a nightgown so sexy she blushed at the table. Papa said that was his gift! I gave Papa a gift certificate from a chichi photography studio good for a family portrait. Jean-Paul got a bottle of Jamaican Punch smell good from Carol's Daughter. He was the type of man who always smelled wonderful, when he wasn't reeking of negative emotions, that is.

Papa Jack gave me a pair of good walking shoes to prowl Tremé in. They weren't as divalicious as I'd usually go for, but they'd keep my feet happy. Mama said she'd give me my gift when we got home. Jean-Paul gave me—surprise—a beautifully bound copy of *The Interior Castle*, which I'd start as soon as I went to bed.

Jean-Paul picked at his food. He had sat too far away for me to touch him with the hope of getting a sense of what he was going through. I had to use my intuition. What I discerned was that the war with himself he'd told me about had become so bloody he was battle-fatigued. His mask had slipped so far off, the parents expressed their concern. He waved their questions away.

"I am fine. It's true." He'd taken to saying "it's true" from me, and my speech was now seasoned with some sassy French.

"Go home and get some sleep. *Très bien?*" He had a faraway look about him, and I was worried for him, too.

"That is a good idea, *ma soeur.*" He stood, looked us all over, and said, *"Je vous aimez, ma famille."* I love you, family. This time I didn't hold my tongue.

"I love you, too, Jean-Paul."

He stared at me for a moment, nodded, and left.

After Jean-Paul's departure the parents looked like a couple of canary-swallowing cool cats.

"What is up with you two?"

Mama looked like she had a delicious secret and couldn't decide if she should share it or not, but it was Christmas in New Orleans. Papa Noël and the Baby Jesus were generous, and Mama couldn't hold a secret tonight if it had a handle on it.

She pulled a red envelope out of her purse. "I thought we should give you this, and I want to ask you to forgive me for meddling."

I took the envelope from her and opened it. Inside was a ticket to a Christmas Day jazz extravaganza to benefit a home for abandoned children.

"Thanks, y'all. This is nice." All I needed was to go listen to music that made me think of Francis. They might as well have bought me the rope to hang myself with.

Papa Jack shook his head. "It'll be quite a lineup, Em. The brothers Marsalis will be there. That alone is worth the price of the ticket. And they're introducing a young man they think will be a superstar. His name is Francis Peace Rivera."

"Francis is going to be in town tomorrow?"

"That's what a little bird told us," Mama said.

I don't know how they got such information, but I was thankful for the birds of the air. I hugged the parents for a long time.

Chapter Thirty-two

I don't need to tell you that I was a nervous wreck. Thank God for that *Interior Castle* book. It was only thing that kept me from going through my closet and setting fire to all my inadequate clothes. And where in the heck was I supposed to get an outfit on Christmas Day? Mama was too short for me to share clothes with. I had to go inside my castle, find a comfortable chair in the room of self-knowledge, and drag my confidence and courage out—and whatever else I could take with me to the concert.

I decided on the red dress Jean-Paul had given me. It was strapless, and a little formal, but with the wrap and some bohemian jewelry I could actually pull off exceptionally fly ingénue. Fortunately, I had those kinds of accessories. So I stressed, dressed, and that afternoon took a cab—Papa insisted—to the Roosevelt, a swanky, gloriously-restored-to-its-original-richly-detailed-fabulousness hotel.

The place was so beautiful, I wanted to run across its elaborate tiled floor, climb its gold columns, or swing on one of its many crystal chandeliers. But I had to restrain myself. This was not the time to fall in love with a hotel. I had a man to make amends to.

I could hardly make it through the concert. Thank goodness Francis performed early in the show. His music relaxed and strengthened me for my task, but they'd have to restore the roof again, because Francis tore it off. He was a mega hit, and I hoped he felt as victorious as he should have, and that I wouldn't ruin the night for him.

There was a VIP meet and greet afterward. Mama and Papa's generosity ensured I had one of the very expensive golden tickets. I hugged the wall like I was a little brown mouse, giving Francis ample time to enjoy his praise. When the crowd had thinned and he stood alone—which took a really long time—I took a deep breath, put my swagger on, and sauntered over to him like I owned the world.

His attention was elsewhere. He didn't see me approach until I was very near him. Oh, my. He'd had as difficult a time as I had. He looked thin and exhausted. Poor baby. He had no parents to comfort him during his heartbreak like I did. I didn't even know where he'd been staying.

He froze when he saw me and took in all the fabulousness of Emme all growed up. If the look of adoration on his face was any indicator, he liked what he saw.

I realized I was still wearing the engagement ring he'd given. I so didn't sell it and give the proceeds to the poor. When we broke up, I didn't have my job, and I'd reasoned that I *was* the poor. But the room of self-knowledge revealed I kept the ring because I still wanted to marry him.

I hid my hands behind my back, and my wrap slipped, revealing more boobage than Francis had ever seen on baby-doll T-shirt girl. His eyes widened.

"Emme?" A question.

"Hi!" I said, far too chipper, like I was his waitress and about to ask him if he'd like to order his drink. My nervous laugh was the kind that slips out when you're totally discombobulated.

"How are you . . . uh, *Frank?*" I wasn't sure if we were on terms that allowed me to call him Francis.

"Emme. Wow."

Wow, indeed. This was so awkward.

"You sounded amazing. As usual." Could I have been any more trite?

"You *look* amazing. As usual." He was really never great at flirting, but I liked his improvisation on my hackneyed line.

We stared at each other, and I wondered if my face mirrored the complicated dance of emotions I saw in his.

"Um . . ." Then came my nervous titter again. I took another deep breath. "I was wondering if I could buy you a cup of coffee. Or maybe a glass of wine if you prefer."

He cocked his head. "How are you going to do that? You're eighteen."

"I look older."

"Yes, you do today." He hesitated. "I'm busy. Sorry."

"What about later?"

"I can't. But it was great to see you."

That changed things. I'd have to blurt out my apology right here. I glanced around the room. Not many people were left, and there was no one else waiting to talk to Francis. Thank God I'd spent some time in that room of self-knowledge. It made me a much more honest woman.

"Frank, I am truly sorry. I misled you. I let you think something was going on with Jean-Paul and me, and it was, just not what you thought."

He looked away, then back at me. "Don't do this to me now, Emme."

"I have to. Please?"

He nodded and let me go on.

"It wasn't panic attacks that you had when you were eighteen," In said. "That was you coming into your ability as a sensitive, and it may have had a lot to do with you going to live in the home of an exorcist. The same thing happened to me when I came here."

I told him about the attack, and the walk with Jean-Paul. I was excruciatingly honest and even told him that I indeed had an indelible connection to Jean-Paul. I had no control over it. It just was. And then I got to what was most important.

"When I was sexually assaulted, I lost faith in myself. I'm afraid you were collateral damage on my journey of finding out who I really am."

The golden light in his eyes softened. He was listening from his own interior castle. And surely God was talking to him.

"I want to ask you to forgive me for being a foolish little girl." My eyes misted. "You didn't deserve to be treated so badly, repeatedly."

I don't know why I was crying. I guess it was because I knew it was over. Free will had changed the whole picture. Francis was refusing to work with me again, and good for him. Maybe he'd fallen in love with his own stranger in the mirror.

I made a courteous little bow to him, wiped my eyes, and gave a lingering last look at those gold-flecked eyes. "*Adieu,* my beloved. I wish you very well."

A sob tore from my throat, and I put my hand over my mouth and turned to flee.

He grabbed me by my left hand and pulled me back toward him. "Wait."

I know he felt the ring. Maybe I'd flashed it by accident.

I was so busted, but the ring was his, and he'd do like the little poor man, his namesake, and sell it to give the proceeds to the poor. Or maybe it would go to whoever his new girlfriend would be: probably one of those pretty little wavy-haired high-yellow girls who made my life miserable as a kid by calling me "blackie."

I hadn't said anything when he'd swung me around. But he did.

"About that coffee . . ."

Chapter Thirty-three

I couldn't help but think he was testing me when he asked if I minded if we ordered room service from his room.

"I'm tired. It was a long show." He smirked. "My ex-fiancée used to trip about that kind of thing, except for when *she* needed to do something like that."

"That's cool with me, as long as there's a fireplace," I said with a wicked grin.

He got a big laugh out of that one. "I don't think I'd flatter myself if I were you."

"Flatter myself? It'd be me in the bed of roses."

Emme Vaughn was a grown woman now. Francis didn't know what to do with me. Suffice it to say, the elevator ride up was very quiet, him being as bashful as a little boy.

"Sorry. No fireplace," he said as he opened the door.

"Pity."

"I guess you'll have to be a good kid," he said. He closed the door behind us and locked it.

His record company had sprung for a superior guest room, which smelled of leather from the chair stationed at the desk and two bench ottomans. A faint fragrance of vanilla and lavender hung in the air.

The room had two double beds divided by a shining mahogany chest of drawers. Ritzy brocade duvets were folded at the feet of both. In the corner, a cushy damask-print chair invited guests to come and sit a spell, and a modest-sized flat-screen television was mounted on the wall.

With a graceful sweep of his arm Francis motioned toward the chair. "Have a seat, Emme. I'll call room service and get us some coffee." Then with exaggerated surprise he exclaimed. "Oh, look! There's a minibar in here! Let's see what's inside."

I was sure this was a test now. One he thought was hilarious.

"Hmmm," he said, crouched at the entertainment center. "What do you know? It has wine. There's a *wicked* Bordeaux if you like a full-bodied red. Or you can have a Pinot Blanc if you prefer white, but I wouldn't bother with it. Not in that dress." He turned to me. "How about champagne? It looks like a good year."

I put my sexy-shoed feet on the ottoman, giving him an outstanding view of my long legs. "I'll have what you're having, Frank."

He shut the door of the minibar with a smirk, picked up the phone, and ordered two peppermint white chocolate mochas. Already I was winning.

They arrived ten small-talk-filled minutes later.

We drank our coffee in awkward silence, him sitting on the bed. Occasionally he punctuated the quiet with a barb. I could take it. It was part of my atonement.

Finally he got serious. "Why did you come up?"

"Do you want the truth?"

He paused. "I'm not sure."

"That's understandable. Why did you ask me up?"

"You're still wearing my ring."

"Because I'm going to marry you, *Francis*."

"Call me Frank," he said with a mischievous gleam in his golden eyes.

He finished his cuppa Joe and went on to a bottle

of water before he repeated his question. "So, why did you come up here. Seriously?"

"Seriously? I wanted to make out."

He laughed again and raked his hand through his hair. "I'm not interested."

That stung. "Do you want me to leave now?"

"Yes. I do."

I stood in my towering heels. He was a gentleman, but this time he didn't get up from where he sat. I tossed my wrap over my shoulder. "You know where I live. I hope to see you soon."

He didn't ask for his ring back. I moved closer to the door, but his voice stopped me. "What makes you think I'd even consider marrying you now?"

"You're still in love with me."

"What's that got to do with anything?"

Again, "Do you want me to leave?"

"I already said yes."

"Fine. I'll be going now."

Before I could even turn he asked, "In your wildest dreams, when would you be doing this marrying me you insist you're going to do. Three years? Five? Fifteen or twenty?"

"You got any priest friends in town you can call in a favor to? Maybe we could skip all that Pre-Cana prep work. We'll just do it on Saturday and bungle along whether or not the marriage is good."

"It might be good."

"I guess we'll see on Saturday."

He stretched his long legs out and crossed his ankles. "Or not."

Now I was tired of playing games. Without responding I walked all the way to the door, knowing he didn't want me to leave. But he didn't call out again, and there was only so much punishment I was willing to take at one time.

I put my hand on the doorknob. The problem was, I didn't want to leave either. I'd make one last effort before I left. And if it didn't work there was a strong possibility that he'd continue to talk his self out of us.

I turned on my stilettos. Put on a big, brave smile and said, "You do want to make out, don't you?"

I guess he had his own brand of brave. With those golden eyes smoldering like fire he gave me a sly smile and said, "Come to daddy." And held out his arms to welcome me.

∞

I'm not sure what I expected. For all my talk of being all growed up, when I reached the bed and sat down I felt shy. I was glad we didn't waste much time with words. He inclined himself toward me. I met him halfway. Our kiss was tentative, but not afraid. It was as if our lips were getting to know each other again. We took our time.

Soon he put his hands at my waist. I knew this man. Jean-Paul was right. When you spend time with God deep in that interior castle, you do gain insight, not just into yourself, or God, but your loved ones, and he was loved. He would never lay me on the bed, grope me, or allow us to get too fired up. He just slid his hands across the silk and circled my waist. I had never felt safer in his arms.

Francis pulled away abruptly, confusing me so much I couldn't even form the words to ask, "What's wrong?"

A look of deep apprehension pinched in his face. "Take off that dress."

Aw, shoot! Maybe I wasn't the only one who had changed. "Excuse me?"

"Something's wrong with it."

"This is a joke, right? You're still testing me."

He shook his head. "I know this sounds crazy, but that dress has some bad juju on it."

He really was serious. He stood and paced the floor before pulling an Orthodox prayer rope out of his pocket, probably a gift from Mother Nicole. The Jesus prayer rattled rapidfire from his mouth.

"Lord Jesus Christ, son of the living God, have mercy on me a sinner." Again and again, until he stopped still.

His voice sounded like he was going into his castle within to hear God. "Tell me about that dress."

"Jean-Paul brought it to me. He was trying to cheer me up, because I was mad depressed after we broke up. I have no idea where he got it. I went to a party in it. The party was weird. Maybe that's it."

My own words came rushing back to me: I have no idea where he got it. It echoed what Papa Jack had said about Celestine's white dress. No one in her life knew where it came from.

Oh, man! Those crazy parties! Jean-Paul had said they had different themes. I went to a red party. It was so possible that Celestine could have gone to a white one.

I closed my eyes and imagined the photographs. Every detail was burned in my memory. Jane Doe was right! I had been looking at the biggest clue the whole time. That's why Celestine banged on the photos that showed the dress. Hers had Audrey Hepburn elegance; something a man with expensive, immaculate taste would buy.

"Francis, I think Jean-Paul might have had something to do with Celestine's death. You must have picked up on it when you touched this dress!"

I was a little salty with myself. I touched that dress, and I had nothin'. Then I realized Jean-Paul had given me the answer to even that. He told me to act like I was just a body: a perfect way to keep me out of my castle, and the wisdom inside it.

Lord, Jesus Christ, son of the living God, have mercy on me, a sinner indeed!

Chapter Thirty-four

I made haste to borrow Francis's cell phone to call Jean-Paul. He picked up on the first ring.

"What is this phone number, Emme?" This before I said hello.

"I need to ask you something, J-P."

"Three-one-three area code. Could that be the metro Detroit area?"

"Whose dress is this?"

"She was your size. Not the shoes. Those I purchased. You have big feet."

"Okay, let's focus here. Jean-Paul, did you have something to do with Celestine's murder?"

"You let him touch you."

"He touched the dress! All he did was put his arms around my waist."

"You kissed him."

"I love him. You know this."

A bellowing laugh sounded out of the iPhone, so shrill and full of pain that for a moment, I moved the phone away from my ear, until I heard him speak again. "I don't have anything to lose now."

"What are you talking about, J-P?"

"I don't know what's going to happen, so I want you to hear my confession."

This did not sound good.

"I didn't kill Tina, but like me, she was ambitious. She'd do anything to get what she wanted, and what she wanted was fame."

So much for the pious girl who never kissed a boy. "Go on."

He heaved a breathy sigh into the phone. "I took her to one of Boko's parties. You may have guessed they are by invitation only. Only the people there know they exist, but many of them are powerful players in this city. That is why no one knew where she had gone, and why no one had ever seen the dress."

"Aw, man, J-P."

"After she met him at a 'fire' party, she wanted to get something from him, and he has a lot. So she asked to come to another one, the white party, and then she went to be alone with him. He took her up to his inner chamber. I had no idea what was going on. Then she came up missing. That wasn't like her. She may have wanted what she did to a fault, but she talked to me on a regular basis."

"Was she your lover?"

"I don't sleep with jail bait."

"Why didn't you go to the police?"

"Because something started happening to me. It was just before you arrived."

He frustrated me. "Dude! What was it? I don't have time to guess."

"May I say? You were a revelation. You came at exactly the right time to clarify what I needed to do. Once I told you that you are my other. You are the perfect person needed for me to complete this task. I must see you. Meet me at Boko's plantation house."

"When?"

"Come at once."

"What is this about, Jean-Paul?"

"I'm going to kill that S.O.B." He did not use the letters. "I want you to watch him die like the dog he is."

"Jean-Paul, you're talking crazy."

"I'll see you there. If you bring him with you, you will regret it."

He hung up his phone and didn't answer again.

∾

I told Francis everything he said.

"Wait a minute," he said. "Did you say the guy's name is Bokor?"

I shook my head vigorously. "No, he introduced me to the guy as Boko."

"Last name?"

"He didn't give me a last name."

He prowled around the room like a caged animal until he brightened and snapped his fingers. "I've got it. Boko is not a name. It's a title. It's short for Bokor, like I thought."

"What is it?"

"A bokor is a sorcerer. He does stuff for money that you don't even want to think about. Listen, X. Bokors are the kind of people that scare voodoo practitioners, because they do things that are way too dark for them."

"I joked with Jean-Paul that the party was Dante's Inferno. It was ka-rayzee. I've got to figure out how to get to that house."

"I'm taking you."

"There are two problems, Francis: Jean-Paul said if you came with me, I'd regret it, and I have no idea exactly where it is."

He thought for a moment before he grabbed the keys to the Camry. "Let's go. I'm going to find that house the same way I find you. I'm gonna go and see where God takes us."

"You totally rock, Francis."

"I've got my own confession to make. I was happy to help those kids in that home, but I begged like crazy to be a part of this concert at the last minute. I sent the ticket to your folks. I came here to be with you. Merry Christmas, Emme."

I hugged his neck. "Merry Christmas." And we got out of there fast.

～

If I had any doubts about anyone's ability to follow the Spirit, Francis dispelled them. He did exactly what he said: got in the car, listened, and drove. In forty minutes or so I could see Boko's house in the distance. "That's it."

Francis sped down the road.

His phone rang, but he was too deep within his castle to be bothered. The caller was insistent. It would be more distracting to let the phone ring and ring than to answer it. I snatched it up from the console and recognized our phone number on the caller ID.

"Mama?" I answered.

"Yes, baby," she said. "I have something important to tell you."

"What is it?"

"The dream. I just had it, and I saw more terrifying things than I ever have. You are about to experience one of the most evil presences you've ever known."

"I know that, Mama."

"The man who is called Boko is the man who raped me. He is powerful beyond belief. He's diabolically possessed and irrevocably full of evil, but he is just a man, Emme. There are only so many laws of nature he can violate without consequences."

I pressed my back into the seat, trying to wrap my head around the fact that the most vile, repugnant human being that I had ever met was my father. It sickened me. I rolled the window down.

"Thank you for fortifying the house, baby, because I'm going to be here doing warfare on your behalf. Prayer changes things, and it's powerful. Don't be afraid."

"So this is how we'll take him down together."

"I was given the easiest job, Emme. Fight the good fight, my courageous warrior. And choose life when you are asked to."

Her words puzzled me, but I didn't ponder them long.

"Okay, Mama. I have to go. Keep praying." I hung up his phone and set it back on the console.

Francis looked at me. "Did I hear you right?"

"Boko is my father. It all makes sense. Only a very powerful sorcerer could do the things he did with such deadly results."

"We're almost there, baby. I'm here. We're going to accomplish what God sent you here to do. I've got your back with an Uzi."

"I'm counting on it, Francesco."

∾

Boko's house had no valet service now. I guess even evil sorcerers let the help take Christmas Day off. Nothing surprised me in New Orleans. Boko probably went to church last night.

We sped up his endless driveway, jumped out of the car, and while Francis ran I tottered in those outrageous heels. This was definitely not my Exorsistah uniform, but I had to roll with it.

Francis waited for me at the door. Fortunately it was unlocked, a gift from Jean-Paul, no doubt. He was inside. I could feel him. No one was dead yet that I could discern.

The house was enormous. "Francis, you're going to have to use your intuition to get us to where they are."

He took my hand and without further delay almost dragged me up to the very top floor.

All I could hear was the click of my heels on the hardwood floor. I yanked at his hand and he stopped, but he didn't look happy about it. Brotha was like a hound dog sniffing out the men. I undid those stupid double straps and took off my kicks.

"Hurry."

"I'm trying!"

Barefoot, I could keep up with Francis, and we raced to a room at the end of a long corridor.

"They're in here," he said.

"I have no game plan, Francis."

"It's inside you, Emme. Don't doubt that."

I remembered Miss Jane, and her commission. She said a lot of lives would be saved if Mama and I took him down. Mama would do her part in prayer, but Miss Jane never said exactly what I was supposed to do. Or did she?

I thought of Ms. Mary, who told me it was time to put on my big-girl panties. I'd sat in that hotel room with Francis, flirting for all I was worth, listening to him talk about choosing wine. And I thought that was something! But this was going to be the most adult thing I'd ever done.

The door was cracked. I kicked it wide open with my bare foot. That had absolutely no real power, but a woman sometimes has to make a grand entrance, if only to shore herself up.

I was glad I'd put on that little bit of swagger, because the room I charged into was the very one I'd dreamed. Crazy symbols, sigils, diabolical signatures were written all over. This was Boko's lair: the seat of his power. This is where I saw someone die. The question was, which one of us was the lamb?

We literally formed a triangle: Francis and me at one point, Jean-Paul at another, and Big Nasty at the other.

Jean-Paul spoke first. "I told you not to bring him."

"Sorry, dude," Francis answered. "Emme and I are in this together."

Jean-Paul's magnetism pulled at me. He was powerful, and I used all I had in me to resist him. Grabbing Francis by the arm, I felt like I was in a tug-of-war. One man held me with his strong body and steadfast love, the other yanked at me with his strong, willful, hungry spirit.

I screamed at Jean-Paul. "Stop it! What do you want from me?"

"I told you I always get what I want."

Now Boko spoke. "Let her go, darling son. She can't beat us with ten of that boy."

I looked Jean-Paul full in the face, and was so stunned I couldn't say the words.

Francis could. "He's your brother. Look at him, Emme. That's why you connected with him."

Sure enough, there it was, my own face in his.

I had a whole arsenal of warfare prayers available to me, and one of the most prayerful men I have ever met by my side, but I had the strangest sense that none of it was going to work in here.

How can that be? My prayers worked against the wicked demon Asmodeus. Boko can't have that much power.

Another voice spoke inside of me: a woman with an enchanting accent, not unlike Father Miguel's. "This is a different kind of battle," Saint Teresa of Avila urged, "go within."

Quiet yourself, Emme. You have to be able to hear. Where do I go in the castle of many rooms? God, help me.

A single very soft prayer arose in my soul, Psalm 131, one of the most gentle prayers I'd ever known:

O Lord, my heart is not lifted up, my eyes are not raised too high; I do not occupy myself with things too great and too marvelous for me. But I have calmed and quieted my soul, like a weaned child with its mother; my soul is like the weaned child that is within me.

I didn't understand—did God want me to grow up, only to be a child again? So I stayed quiet. Francis didn't say a word.

Boko talked to his son. "Why didn't you tell me she was the one I've always wanted since I took her *delish* mama?"

I rocked back on my heels. *Quiet, Emme.*

Jean-Paul: "I wanted to see if you would recognize her."

He laughed. Some of his words came out in a long drawl. "I recognize her now-wah. Whhhhy don't you lay her down on the altar right he-ah?"

I didn't move.

"Jean-Paul. Did you he-ah me, son?"

"I have a surprise for you, Boko. Something happened to me when your baby girl arrived. We were in church. I wanted nothing to do with it, but I didn't want her to know that, so I sat down, and she begin to pray. And the next thing you know, my most painful buried memory came to fore, and I saw your ugly face as plain as day.

"You killed my mother, you filthy, gluttonous monster, and I'm going to kill *you* and take everything you have. We have the same DNA but you lack discipline and appeal. I'll run this empire better than you could conceive of. All of this will be mine, mine and Emme's."

Jean-Paul pulled out a silver dagger from the waistband of his pants. I wondered who would be the lamb.

That voice from deep inside, the one I know is God, began to murmur a message to me.

Talk to your brother.

I didn't argue with God this time.

"Jean-Paul! Don't do this. You mentioned DNA. Your mother's evidence files may have some DNA preserved. You can make him pay in another way. He can go to jail for the rest of his life, not just for your mother's murder, but for Tina's, too."

"I like my way better." Jean-Paul stopped talking to Boko, the knife still in his hand. Now he spoke to me.

"I want you to help me, Emme. You are my sister. You can be powerful beyond your wildest dreams. Together we can run all of New Orleans. All you have to do is help me. I won't let you get your hands dirty, my beloved. And I will give you everything a woman needs or wants: everything. All of this can be yours," Jean Paul said, just like the devil told Jesus, but I wanted nothing to do with Boko's evil empire.

"I'd have everything except God. I want him more than all this."

"I'll give you a moment to think about it," Jean-

Paul said. Having dismissed my refusal, he charged at Boko with the knife.

Here's where it all went crazy, or rather, crazier. Francis rushed Jean-Paul to keep him from killing Boko. He wrestled the dagger from my brother's hand.

You wouldn't think a big man like Boko could move so fast. But he went for the knife and I stood there trying to figure out how to be a weaned child, completely reliant on my Father God. I was so confused. Wasn't my lesson here to be a grown woman, too?

Boko got the knife, and I stayed quiet. I thought he'd go after the guys, trying to get to Jean-Paul, who had threatened his entire existence. But this is the man who lusted for me when I was still in my mother's womb. The wicked demon he'd bonded with, Asmodeus, was gone, but Boko was just as dangerous. Francis was right. There are some things in this world that are scarier than demons.

Before I could even process what happened he had me by my long white hair.

"I'm going to have you."

"I'd rather die," I said, and spit in his face. He yanked my neck back with the knife in his hand. And God said, "Be still."

I do not occupy myself with things too great and too marvelous for me.

Boko raised the knife, and just before he struck my neck, Celestine appeared. She yanked my head out of his hand. The knife plunged into my chest instead of slitting my throat. It slashed right through the markings Saint Michael had said was the seal of God on my chest.

Chapter Thirty-five

I remember the shock I felt. How the dagger burned going in and broke through two of my ribs. Francis grabbed Boko by the neck. I held my chest and felt warm blood ooze out, then spurt.

Then everything went white and beautiful. I floated out of the body that I had just begun to learn to love. Below I could see Boko lying on the ground. Francis desperately applied pressure to my chest. Jean-Paul stood over him, watching.

"Hello, dear heart," a voice behind me said. I turned. It was Miss Jane. She didn't have a cigarette.

"This is really nice," I said. "I feel so happy here."

"For you this is a happy place."

"Is it time to go?"

She was quiet for a moment. "I don't want you to come yet, my dear girl."

I shook my head. "Everybody down there is gonna be all right. This is so much better. I don't have any bad memories. Everybody is forgiven. All is well."

"You're going to get married, Emme, just as I said."

I wanted to feel sad that she didn't want me to stay, but I couldn't. Saint Michael came and stood beside her. He spoke to me. "Hello, my Emme."

"Hey, Brother. Did you come to take me to Jesus? I really want to see him."

"I will take you if you insist upon it. It is your choice, but you must know that you do not have to come right now. If you choose to return, your brother, who is indelibly connected to you, will sense your decision, and he will help you. Love will compel him, and my Emme, he needs an act of pure love to cover a multitude of his sins. But if you do not choose to stay, he will release you, with sorrow. It is up to you."

"It's so peaceful here."

"It is time to put on your big-girl panties and choose. Heaven or earth?"

It sounded so weird hearing Saint Michael say "big-girl panties." I was going to say "I choose heaven." I mean, earth life kinda sucked most of the time for me, but before I replied Miss Jane held up her finger, urging me to be quiet.

"Emme, before you tell him what you've chosen, take one look at Francis, please."

I squinted through the white until I could see him. He was crying. I'd never seen Francis cry except at his father's funeral, and then it had been very restrained. But he was bawling, right in front of Jean-Paul.

"He just lost his father a few weeks ago. Remember, you told yourself you wouldn't hurt him again. Free will will make the difference in the outcome here. Choose life, Emme, like your mother urged you to do. She's praying you will at this very moment.

"What will happen to Jean-Paul if you're not there to be his Monica?" Jane said. "He doesn't need you praying for him here. He needs you beside him, Emme. Now you may choose, dear heart."

And I did.

Chapter Thirty-six

I woke up in a thin place between heaven and earth. It is a place where there are good spirits and bad spirits, and everything in between.

When I came back to consciousness, it wasn't Francis who had his hands on my chest. It was my brother, and it felt like sunshine came out of his hands. My broken ribs didn't hurt anymore. My heart wound had sealed. My brother had found within himself the power to choose love over hate.

Boko was dead. His excesses had finally worn his

heart of flesh out. When Francis pulled him away he had tried to run, stumbled, had a heart attack, and died. No one expected *that*. I was just glad one of my lovies didn't have the scourge of murdering someone, even a person as evil as Boko, on them.

I walked out of that plantation house without a scratch. But the dress was ruined. The seal God placed on me was gone. I guess I wouldn't need it anymore.

The next Saturday morning, before God, my mama, my papa, and a priest who owed Francis a favor, I married the man who was my destiny, while my brother rested in a psychiatric hospital. I bombard heaven with prayers for him, and visit often.

Now my husband and I live in the duplex right next door to my parents, in an artist community called Tremé. In my new hometown, there are good spirits, and bad spirits, and everything in between.

Sometimes I can see these lost souls. Sometimes I can't. At times they ask for my help, and I serve them well; I do my job. I am the Exorsistah. I chase demons. Demons chase me. Most of the time, I beat the brakes off them, in Jesus's name. In this thin and beautiful place, I have found my happily ever after.

Amen, and amen.

Don't miss the first book in the exciting
Exorsistah series

THE EXORSISTAH

Available now from
Pocket Books

When we got back inside, I could almost see the tension like I could demons. Francis happily chatted while we trekked down the hall—like I'm all ready to sign up for whatever.

He noticed my lack of enthusiasm.

"Can we just *talk* about the *work*? No pressure. I never had a friend interested in this stuff that wasn't an old white person."

"You still don't have one."

He ignored my dis.

"I'm hoping the bishop will expedite the process of approving the exorcism of this girl, or Father Miguel is gonna be too sick to perform the rite. Plus she's in bad shape. Her parents are *through*. They've done all they could with the little they have. Can't get much help for anything when you're broke and living in the hood."

He spoke so fast it sounded almost like he said it all in one breath. "Father Rivera and I don't agree on a lot of things. Actually, we don't agree on most things. I believe in the priesthood of *all* believers. He stands by tradition with a big 'T.' And I see his point. But you know, God works through and then beyond tradition. I'm trying to figure out what God is doing next. What will the next-generation exorcist look like?"

He squeezed my hand. "Maybe they'll be an *exorsistah* in the future."

"As long as it ain't me."

"Stay open, Chiara. I had to have met you for a reason."

"It ain't *that* reason."

He pulled me into the living room, halting our discussion.

I tried to subtly pull my hand out of his, but he wouldn't let go. I didn't like that feeling. He knew I was a runaway. He said he could *see* what had happened with the men in my past. I thought he'd understand that I don't like feeling like somebody is forcing me to do something. Especially when it comes to touching. I was tired of being manipulated by men, and I didn't want somebody holding my hand when I didn't want it to be held. But I didn't want to cut a fool in front of his people. I had to talk to my inner self—"He's holding your hand. That's all"—to keep from goin' off on him.

He leaned over and whispered in my ear, "Chill, Emme. I know what your concerns are. I'm showing you that I've got you. It's a unity move. That's all."

I relaxed my hand and stopped resisting him.

Father Rivera and Mother Nicole were watching us. I couldn't have been more self-conscious if I'd stepped onto the stage during amateur night at the Apollo.

Mother Nicole sat by the old man on the sofa. I thanked God for that woman. Those hazel eyes shone with compassion for me, in contrast to Father Rivera's suspicious gaze. His eyes were light, too, almost like Francis's, but more the color of amber. The kind you see bugs trapped for thousands of years in. I imagined myself stuck in those hard eyes.

I nodded a greeting to them. The old man nodded in return. Mother Nicole said in stark contrast to our brusque mannerisms, "Hello, Emme. How did you sleep, lovie?"

"I slept fine, Mother Nicole. Did your prayers go okay?"

Her face lit up like she didn't expect me to ask about that. "They sure did. I prayed for you, too. God assured me He had you in the palm of His hand."

"Thanks."

I turned my focus to the ground because something about the tenderness in her voice and eyes touched my heart when she said that. Man, I felt so weary. But I didn't want them to see me go all soft, especially the old man.

"Make yourself comfortable, Emme," Francis said, and he gestured to the sofa next to Mother Nicole. He stood in the middle of the room and put his spin on my being there.

"Father Miguel, once again, this is Emme Vaughn. She's cool people, but things are a little rough for her. I've told you both a little about her, how I met her at Walgreens last night. I told you about the housing trouble she has right now and also about the extraordinary gift she has to see into the spirit world." He turned to me. "Emme, maybe you can tell them more about it."

I cut my eyes at him.

The old man spoke. "Do you have to coach her through this? Can't she speak for herself?"

Mother Nicole warned, "Father Miguel . . ."

But he tore right into me, and not about being homeless. "What is this so-called gift, young lady?"

I yanked on my emotional armor. "I never said I had a gift. Holla at yo' boy about that."

"My boy?"

Mother Nicole answered, "She means your *friend*, Miguel."

Father Miguel gave me another verbal nudge. Or push. "Come, come now. Don't be modest. I don't think Frank would have brought you here if he didn't have some ridiculous notion about you being involved in our *work*. Or is there some other reason he had you in his bed, Miss Vaughn?"

Mother Nicole said more firmly this time, *"Miguel!"*

I decided to let that go for Mother Nicole's sake. Francis could tell that man was tickin' me off though. He tried to reassure me with his eyes. "Just tell him how it works, Emme, so he can drop the subject and we can get on to the social justice stuff we're supposed to be about because we're followers of Christ." He gave Father Rivera a hard look and me a kind one. "Okay, Emme?"

I addressed Father Rivera. "I already told him I don't know how it works. It's like the veil between heaven and earth gets lifted, and I can see into spirit worlds. Why or how, I couldn't tell you. Why don't you ask God? Ain't y'all 'sposed to be tight like that?"

"You watch your tone with me, Miss Vaughn. This is *my* house."

"With all due respect, Father Rivera, I left your

house a few minutes ago. I'm only here because Francis begged me to come back. And he said we weren't gon' deal with this."

Father Miguel paled. "He told you his name is Francis?"

I decided not to give him all our secrets, and hoped Francis hadn't. "How else would I know it?"

He gave Francis a withering stare, which bro' ignored like he did a good many of my questions.

"What else did he tell you?"

"That I could get some help here. Apparently, he was wrong."

Mother Nicole intervened. "This isn't a war between you and Emme, Miguel. She's just a teenager, and she needs help. She doesn't deserve your completely unacceptable contempt. And Emme, Father Miguel isn't a foster parent intent on exploiting you. He has concerns because he doesn't know you. That's understandable. You may want to soften that edge of yours."

God, forgive me.

I felt bad. My mama raised me to respect my elders, but this man tripped on me from the first moment he looked at me, and my nerves were frayed. "I'm sorry," I muttered, but I meant it.

If Father Rivera felt bad, he didn't offer a word of apology to let anybody in the room know it.

Whatever.

Mother Nicole gave me her attention. "So, Emme, it seems God wills this to happen as He sees fit?"

I shrugged again. I'm sure I looked as sullen and surly as I felt. I didn't want to talk about this. "I guess."

She rocked back against the cushions and adjusted herself. "I wonder if the spiritual disciplines would help her tune in to it more? Sharpen her spiritual antennae, so to speak."

This idea seemed to excite Francis. "That's what I wondered, too!" He caught himself and tamed that enthusiasm. "But she doesn't want to get involved with that ministry. I can't blame her, but I couldn't help but think if she did want to work with us, part of her training should be the classic disciplines. I thought we'd give her the total package: physical, spiritual, and emotional. It would be a whole new thing. Something we've never done."

"Too bad I ain't doing it," I said.

Concern shadowed Mother Nicole's face. "I believe her instincts are spot on, Frankie. I know you think Emme is special, but that doesn't mean she's suitable for the *work*, even if she wanted to do it."

"And I don't," I said.

He kinda blushed. "She *is* special to me, Mama Nic, and not just because she can see the spirit world. As far as the *work* is concerned, her gift . . ." He paused, looking buzzed on this idea of me working with them. "I'm sure we could find a way to integrate it."

Father Rivera broke in, shattering Francis's excitement like somebody pouring ice water on him. "It sounds ridiculous! First of all, you don't know if she really has this gift she says she has."

I sighed like the three of them had a habit of doing. "I ain't say I had no gift. Okay?"

Francis told Father Rivera, "I've seen her operating this gift."

I didn't appreciate them talking about me like I was in the kitchen somewhere with Penny Pop.

Father Rivera turned to me. "You don't know what you saw," he challenged.

I tried to keep my respect in order, when what I really wanted to do was slam him. I held my tongue. Francis didn't.

"But, for real, I saw—"

The old man ranted on at Francis. "And now you parade her around here like it's even possible that she could be an exorcist. What does the Church believe, Frank?"

"That only priests can be exorcists."

"And who can perform exorcisms?"

"Priests, and only with the express permission of a bishop."

"And who does that leave out?"

"That leaves out anyone who isn't a priest with a bishop's blessing, including the teams of believers I've been talking about. And women. And *me*, sir."

For a sick person, Father Rivera didn't have any problem administering a smackdown.

"Then get these romantic notions out of your head. Exorcism is an ugly business. You know that, Frank. I never wanted anything to do with it, myself. It's bad enough that you want to be a priest. Why can't you just enjoy being a young man? Even as insolent as she is, I'd rather you be taking her out to dinner instead of trying to get her involved with casting out demons. Let old men do what old men do. And priests do what priests do."

Mother Nicole jumped in the conversation. "He's right, Frankie. It's not that we don't appreciate you. Father Miguel has needed you in these last few cases more than ever. But she's young, very thin, and unseasoned."

The old man looked me up and down like I was nothing. Less than nothing. He spoke to Francis. "She can't do us any good. That you even considered her should be an affront, even to her."

"She's gifted," he said, tryna stay cool. "I know she's thin. That ain't a sin! She's malnourished from fasting like one of the desert Ammas and not having a place she felt safe enough to eat."

"Then take a few days, feed her, and get her out of here."

Francis thrust his hands in his pockets, shook his head, and smiled, like this was some kind of power game they played at.

He rocked on the heel of his Timbs. "I can take her somewhere, but I'll go with her 'cause she's on my watch now. And *I* don't leave vulnerable sistahs hangin'."

The priest didn't say anything. Dude just scowled at Francis. And me.

Francis turned to me. "I'm thinkin' you can stay as long as you need to, Emme," he said. "The good father didn't say anything against us, so I'ma take that to mean he's for us."

With that he grabbed my hand again, and we made a grand exit.

I followed Francis through the narrow hallway of the bungalow and into a small bedroom he must've been using for storage. Musical instruments propped on or against boxes stacked halfway up the wall: guitars—acoustic and electric—and a couple of basses. Some funky-looking electronic drum. Mama, Papa, and Baby Bear–size amplifiers. Bro' was serious about his music.

"Dang, boy," I said. "You got everything up in this piece."

"Naw. Not everything, but I'm workin' on it."

"How come you don't keep your instruments in your bedroom? From the looks of your room, I wouldn't have even thought you were a musician."

"I sleep in my room. Read. If I took an instrument in there, I'd end up staying up all night."

A bow-back country stool sat in the center of the

room. He pulled it to the side and motioned for me to have a seat.

I sat and watched him get busy, moving from acoustic guitar, to electric, back to acoustic, and finally settle on a bass. He plugged it into an amplifier, strapped it on, and started tuning it.

"Are you about to serenade me, Francis?"

"Naw," he said grinning and tuning, "I might turn you out, *chica*, and then I won't be able to get rid of you."

"Yeah. I see how hard you been tryna get me out your life. You don't wanna go Usher on me."

"I'ma play bass for you."

"I kinda figured that when you strapped the bass on."

"Quiet, sassy girl."

He didn't just play that bass, though. He, like, became one with it. He made that bass an extension of himself, so that the music wasn't coming out of the instrument. He was the instrument. And he didn't stop there.

Aw, man. His music was, like, transcendent. I watched in openmouthed awe as he plunked, plucked, and picked at the strings in a way that must've made the angels jealous. Francis caressed rhythms out of that baby that went right into the secret place in me where only God lived and once had visited. But I couldn't even trip. The sounds of his music took me to heavenly places, and dang, that was just one bass.

When he stopped, the quiet almost offended me.

For a moment I couldn't speak. He searched my face, for what I wasn't sure. I think he was waiting for me to tell him what I thought, but I couldn't find the words.

Finally he said, "Well?"

"I kinda see what you mean about the turning me out thing."

He looked surprised for a moment. Then we both cracked up.

He got back to the bass, but not what he was doing before. He played the scales, repeating the same boring notes over and over.

"How long do you go through those scales?"

"I spend hours at it sometimes," he said. "It's like prayer. You do it long enough, it's just natural when you have to do something deep. Like spiritual warfare."

"Don't start." I shook my head. "Man. That would drive me crazy."

"It drives Father Miguel crazy, too. I started doing it without the amp so he wouldn't have to hear it, but right now, I'm not feelin' the sensitivity to him. At least for a few minutes."

"You play when you get upset, don't you? It's like

that thing you do when somebody is tryna talk to you when you ain't feelin' it. You escape."

"Yeah," he said. "Sometimes I escape into the music in my head. So, it can be double trouble."

"Are you feeling better now?"

"Much better," he said. "Got my God, got my bass, got my exorsistah. A brotha don't need no more than that right now."

I chuckled. "Well, two outta three ain't bad."

Francis said, "What you talkin' about, girl? *God* is with me."

"Father Rivera ain't feelin' no exorsistah."

His fingers continued running scales. "I told you, he thinks I have motivations that I don't have."

"You brought some sistah he don't know nothing about into his home. He probably thinks we're up to no good."

"It's not that. He knows me. If I was gon' do something like that, I'd leave. I wouldn't disrespect his house. This is complicated, Emmy. Don't sweat it."

I could tell he didn't want to talk about it, so I let him play without pressing the issue. He must've wanted to keep me talking though.

"You play any instruments?" he asked.

"I wish. I do a little spoken word to beats. It ain't nothin' like what you doin'. You don't get a chance to do work on that level when you get tossed around a lot. I'm surprised you got to be so good."

"Yeah, well, I got tossed around with my guitar. I put a lot of time into this. And . . ." He looked embarrassed, and maybe a little bashful. "They say I'm a prodigy."

"Are you?"

"I don't know. I understand music. Always did. The language of it. I *speak* music, if you can get that. I've always been that way. It's like how you see in the spirit world. You just do."

"Francis. Don't go there."

I got up from the chair and explored the room while he played. Touched the boxes with names from companies that sell stuff like speakers. Beat boxes. I wondered what he had in those boxes.

My mind kept going back to why I was in that house. I felt a little sad. I knew this wasn't gonna work out. Not for long, no matter how Francis flexed on the old priest.

"He ain't Mr. Nice Guy is he, that Father Rivera?"

He shook his head, and stretched his long legs out in front of him. "He's definitely not easy, but he has his moments."

I sighed, picking up an acoustic guitar. Francis watched me, but not all paranoid like he didn't want me messing around with his stuff. He looked curious.

I strummed a few strings. "Who does he think he is, anyway? Some kind of super priest? He got powers I don't know about?"

"Nope," he said, still playing the scales.

Scales were kinda gettin' on my nerves, too.

He continued, "Those house slippers hide his feet of clay. But I can't knock his experience. He's a heckuva exorcist, and his results are some of the best in the game. I wouldn't be working with him if he was whack. Or pushing for you to do the same."

The more we talked about it, the more I knew my days of hangin' with Francis were numbered.

"He doesn't like me, and I ain't crazy about him. It was a nice try, but he ain't with your plan. It's cool, though."

"No, it's not, Emme."

"I'll stay a couple of days, but I gotta dip after that, Francis."

He stopped his relentless fingering of bass strings. Stood where he was, his golden eyes looking deeply into mine. My breath hitched.

"I want to share so much with you. Teach you the best things I know." He leaned the instrument against a box. "I want to feed you all kinds of healthy food, teach you everything I know about prayer and the spiritual disciplines. I want to train you in martial arts. Even help you get your GED, if you want. I want to make sure you're the baddest thing the kingdom of God has ever seen. Shield you against the nightmares that you've had to live through since you were a little girl. But I can't do that if you leave."

Shoot. That sounded kinda tight. Then something odd dawned on me. "Why would somebody on an exorcist's team need to know martial arts?"

"Like I said, I'm the muscle. It takes a lot of strength and fortitude to work in deliverance ministry. And on the real, I think you'd be hot as a martial artist."

I saw it. In my mind I was not just kickin' *devil* butt. I was kickin' *a whole lotta* butt. Starting with Ray.

Pow! Pow! Bam!

I put me a list together right quick: all the punks I was in foster care homes with that were just like Ray; Father Rivera—though I went easy on him 'cause Francis liked him, and he was sick; the girl who cut a big chunk of my hair out in the crazy house when I was twelve because she was bald-headed and jealous. I could even kick Francis's butt when he got on my nerves. Or even when he didn't. We could be like Daredevil and Electra in the movie, when they were fighting on that playground when they first met.

I got into my butt-kickin' fantasy so deep I heard Francis's voice, but not what he said to me. "I'm sorry. What?"

He had an amused smirk on his pretty face and now stared at me with one eyebrow raised. "Emme?"

"What, Francis?"

"Not only did I tell you my whole vision of the neo-exorcist, I told you my big sob story of getting my GED despite the odds against me, and blah, blah, blah, none of which you heard. You missed me play the violin, while rain fell against the window and a single tear rolled dramatically down my cheek."

I folded my arms across my chest. "I already know exorcisms are physical, and you did *not* cry. It ain't raining, either. I can't enroll in a GED completion program, Francis. They'd find me."

"Emme, I said—which you obviously missed— that I did it on my own, and I'll bet you could, too. Mother Nicole and I could prep you if you stayed. You don't even have to take the test until after your birthday. You don't have to be so scared. It's not like the police are staking out the hood or throwing up roadblocks to find you. You ran away from a foster care home. You're not on the FBI's Most Wanted list."

"I don't care. They found me before, and it can happen again if I ain't careful. This is Inkster. I grew up here. People know me. I ain't tryna go back into foster care thirty-two days before I'm grown. I'll hang with you a few days, but I'm not with the neo-exorcist thing."

"All right, Emme. I said I wouldn't force you to do anything. Where you tryna go when you get legal?"

"That ain't your concern."

He stepped up to me, all manly and fine, making my heart rate rival what I bet that electronic drum of his could do. Got right in my face.

"It's my concern now. You won't be out there on your own if I can help it. I'm offering you room and board and an intensive spiritual journey that will give you skills you can use for the rest of your life, but if you won't accept my offer I'll still see you to safety somewhere else. I had hoped that since you're Jamilla's age, you could help her. I'm not sure how, but I got a feeling she's not telling us everything. Sometimes girls tell other girls what they won't tell anybody else. But she's in God's hands."

My heart dropped so fast to my feet I thought it'd stay there permanently.

Jamilla?

He noticed my expression change. "What is it, Emme? Are you okay?"

Naw. It wasn't Jamilla. Not my girl.

"Jamilla is her name?"

"Yeah."

I searched my mind for anything he might have said about this girl. He mentioned we were the same age. Did he say she lived in Inkster? *Dang.* He hadn't said much about her at all. *Aw man! Why didn't I ask him more questions?*

My mouth went dry, and I swallowed what felt like a rock in my throat. I asked him one of the hardest questions I ever asked anybody, even though it was a simple one. I silently prayed he wouldn't say what had to be impossible.

"What's Jamilla's last name?"

"Jacobs. Oh, snap! What was I thinking? You lived in Inkster. Maybe you know her."

Oh, *snap*, my butt. He had to have thought about it. The town was too little, and I said I grew up here.

I put the guitar down and walked away from Francis and back to the chair. He didn't follow me, but gave me a little space instead of hovering over me.

After some time I finally managed to say, "Jamilla Jacobs was my best friend. Since we were in the first grade."

"Emme, I'm so sorry."

Shoot. I was sorry, too. Because now I was staying for sure. If she was possessed, I was gonna kick that devil's butt. I didn't care what I had to do.